TALES OF
THREE HEMISPHERES

TALES OF
THREE HEMISPHERES

LORD DUNSANY

(EDWARD J. M. D. PLUNKETT)

Serenity
Publishers, LLC
ROCKVILLE, MARYLAND
2009

ISBN: 978-1-60450-700-3

Published by Serenity Publishers
An Arc Manor Company
P. O. Box 10339
Rockville, MD 20849-0339
www.SerenityPublishers.com

Printed in the United States of America/United Kingdom

CONTENTS

From steaming lowlands down by the equator, where monstrous orchids blow, where beetles big as mice sit on the tent-ropes, and fireflies glide about by night like little moving stars, the travelers went three days through forests of cactus till they came to the open plains where the oryx are.

And glad they were when they came to the water-hole, where only one white man had gone before, which the natives know as the camp of Bwona Khubla, and found the water there.

It lies three days from the nearest other water, and when Bwona Khubla had gone there three years ago, what with malaria with which he was shaking all over, and what with disgust at finding the water-hole dry, he had decided to die there, and in that part of the world such decisions are always fatal. In any case he was overdue to die, but hitherto his amazing resolution, and that terrible strength of character that so astounded his porters, had kept him alive and moved his safari on.

7

He had had a name no doubt, some common name such as hangs as likely as not over scores of shops in London; but that had gone long ago, and nothing identified his memory now to distinguish it from the memories of all the other dead but "Bwona Khubla," the name the Kikuyus gave him.

There is not doubt that he was a fearful man, a man that was dreaded still for his personal force when his arm was no longer able to lift the kiboko, when all his men knew he was dying, and to this day though he is dead.

Though his temper was embittered by malaria and the equatorial sun, nothing impaired his will, which remained a compulsive force to the very last, impressing itself upon all, and after the last, from what the Kikuyus say. The country must have had powerful laws that drove Bwona Khubla out, whatever country it was.

On the morning of the day that they were to come to the camp of Bwona Khubla all the porters came to the travelers' tents asking for dow. Dow is the white man's medicine, that cures all evils; the nastier it tastes, the better it is. They wanted down this morning to keep away devils, for they were near the place where Bwona Khubla died.

The travelers gave them quinine.

By sunset the came to Campini Bwona Khubla and found water there. Had they not found water many of them must have died, yet none felt any gratitude to the place, it seemed too ominous, too full of doom, too much harassed almost by unseen, irresistible things.

And all the natives came again for dow as soon as the tents were pitched, to protect them from the last dreams of Bwona Khubla, which they say had stayed behind when the last safari left taking Bwona Khubla's body back to the edge of civilization to show to the white men there that they had not killed him, for the white men might not know that they durst not kill Bwona Khubla.

And the travelers gave them more quinine, so much being bad for the nerves, and that night by the camp-fires there was no pleasant talk; all talking at once of meat they had eaten and cattle that each one owned, but a gloomy silence hung by every fire and the little canvas shelters. They told the white men that Bwona Khubla's city, of which he had thought at the last (and where the natives believed he was once a king), of which he had raved till the loneliness rang with his raving, had settled down all about them; and they were afraid, for it was so strange a city, and wanted more dow. And the two travelers gave them more quinine, for they saw real fear in their faces, and knew they might run away and leave them alone in that place, that they, too, had come to fear with an almost equal dread, though they knew not why. And as the night wore on their feeling of boding deepened, although they had shared three bottles or so of champagne that they meant to keep for days when they killed a lion.

This is the story that each of those two men tell, and which their porters corroborate, but then a Kikuyu will always say whatever he thinks is expected of him.

The travelers were both in bed and trying to sleep but not able to do so because of an ominous feeling. That mournfullest of all the cries of the wild, the hyaena like a damned soul lamenting, strangely enough had ceased. The night wore on to the hour when Bwona Khubla had died three or four years ago, dreaming and raving of "his city"; and in the hush a sound softly arose, like a wind at first, then like the roar of beasts, then unmistakably the sound of motors—motors and motor busses.

And then they saw, clearly and unmistakably they say, in that lonely desolation where the equator comes up out of the forest and climbs over jagged hills,—they say they saw London.

There could have been no moon that night, but they say there was a multitude of stars. Mists had come rolling up at evening about the pinnacles of unexplored red peaks that clustered round the camp. But they say the mist must have cleared later on; at any rate they swear they could see London, see it and hear the roar of it. Both say they saw it not as they knew it at all, not debased by hundreds of thousands of lying advertisements, but transfigured, all its houses magnificent, its chimneys rising grandly into pinnacles, its vast squares full of the most gorgeous trees, transfigured and yet London.

Its windows were warm and happy, shining at night, the lamps in their long rows welcomed you, the public-houses were gracious jovial places; yet it was London.

They could smell the smells of London, hear London songs, and yet it was never the London that they knew; it was as though they had looked on some strange woman's face with the eyes of her lover. For of all the towns of the earth or cities of song; of all the spots there be, unhallowed or hallowed, it seemed to those two men then that the city they saw was of all places the most to be desired by far. They say a barrel organ played quite near them, they say a coster was singing, they admit that he was singing out of tune, they admit a cockney accent, and yet they say that that song had in it something that no earthly song had ever had before, and both men say that they would have wept but that there was a feeling about their heartstrings that was far too deep for tears. They believe that the longing of this masterful man, that was able to rule a safari by raising a hand, had been so strong at the last that it had impressed itself deeply upon nature and had caused a mirage that may not fade wholly away, perhaps for several years.

I tried to establish by questions the truth or reverse of this story, but the two men's tempers had been so spoiled by Africa that they were not up to cross-examination. They would not even say if their camp-fires were still burning. They say that they saw the London lights all round them from eleven o'clock till midnight, they could hear London voices and the sound of the traffic clearly, and over all, a little misty perhaps, but unmistakably London, arose the great metropolis.

After midnight London quivered a little and grew more indistinct, the sound of the traffic began to dwindle away, voices seemed farther off, ceased altogether, and all was quiet once more where the mirage shimmered and faded, and a bull rhinoceros coming down through the stillness snorted, and watered at the Carlton Club.

HOW THE OFFICE OF POSTMAN FELL
VACANT IN OTFORD-UNDER-THE-WOLD

The duties of postman at Otford-under-the-Wold carried Amuel Sleggins farther afield than the village, farther afield than the last house in the lane, right up to the big bare wold and the house where no one went, no one that is but the three grim men that dwelt there and the secretive wife of one, and, once a year when the queer green letter came, Amuel Sleggins the postman.

The green letter always came just as the leaves were turning, addressed to the eldest of the three grim men, with a wonderful Chinese stamp and the Otford postmark, and Amuel Sleggins carried it up to the house.

He was not afraid to go, for he always took the letter, had done so for seven years, yet whenever summer began to draw to a close, Amuel Sleggins was ill at ease, and if there was a touch of autumn about shivered unduly so that all folk wondered.

And then one day a wind would blow from the East, and the wild geese would appear, having left the sea, flying high and crying strangely, and pass till they were no more than a thin black line in the sky like a magical stick flung up by a doer of magic, twisting and twirling away; and the leaves would turn on the trees and the mists be white on the marshes and the sun set large and red and autumn would step down quietly that night from the wold; and the next day the strange green letter would come from China.

His fear of the three grim men and that secretive woman and their lonely, secluded house, or else the cadaverous cold of the dying season, rather braced Amuel when the time was come and he would step out bolder upon the day that he feared than he had perhaps for weeks. He longed on that day for a letter for the last house in the lane, there he would dally and talk awhile and look on church-going faces before his last tramp over the lonely wold to end at the dreaded door of the queer grey house called wold-hut.

When he came to the door of wold-hut he would give the postman's knock as though he came on ordinary rounds to a house of every day, although no path led up to it, although the skins of weasels hung thickly from upper windows.

And scarcely had his postman's knock rung through the dark of the house when the eldest of the three grim men would always run to the door. O, what a face had he. There was more slyness in it than ever his beard could hide. He would put out a gristly hand; and into it Amuel Sleggins would put the letter from China, and rejoice that his duty was done, and would turn and stride away. And the fields lit up before him, but, ominous, eager and low murmuring arose in the wold-hut.

For seven years this was so and no harm had come to Sleggins, seven times he had gone to wold-hut and as often come safely away; and then he needs must marry. Perhaps because she was young, perhaps because she was fair or because she had shapely ankles as she came one day through the marshes among the milkmaid flowers shoeless in spring. Less things than these have brought men to their ends and been the nooses with which Fate snared them running. With marriage curiosity entered his house, and one day as they walked with evening through the meadows, one summer evening, she asked him of wold-hut where he only went, and what the folks were like that no one else had seen. All this he told her; and then she asked him of the green letter from China, that came with autumn, and what the letter contained. He read to her all the rules of the Inland Revenue, he told her he did not know, that it was not right that he should know, he lectured her on the sin of inquisitiveness, he quoted Parson, and in the end she said that she must know. They argued concerning this for many days, days of the ending of summer, of shortening evenings, and as they argued autumn grew nearer and nearer and the green letter from China.

And at last he promised that when the green letter came he would take it as usual to the lonely house and then hide somewhere near and creep to the window at nightfall and hear what the grim folk said; perhaps they might read aloud the letter from China. And before he had time to repent of that promise a cold wind came one night and the woods turned golden, the plover went in bands at evening over the marshes, the year had turned, and there came the letter from China. Never before had Amuel felt such misgivings as he went his postman's rounds, never before had he so much feared the day that took him up to the wold and the lonely house, while snug by the fire his wife looked pleasurably forward to curiosity's gratification and hoped to

have news ere nightfall that all the gossips of the village would envy. One consolation only had Amuel as he
set out with a shiver, there was a letter that day for the
last house in the lane. Long did he tarry there to look at
their cheery faces, to hear the sound of their laughter—
you did not hear laughter in wold-hut—and when the
last topic had been utterly talked out and no excuse for
lingering remained he heaved a heavy sigh and plod-
ded grimly away and so came late to wold-hut.

He gave his postman's knock on the shut oak door,
heard it reverberate through the silent house, saw
the grim elder man and his gristly hand, gave up the
green letter from China, and strode away. There is a
clump of trees growing all alone in the wold, desolate, mournful, by day, by night full of ill omen, far off
from all other trees as wold-hut from other houses.
Near it stands wold-hut. Not today did Amuel stride
briskly on with all the new winds of autumn blowing
cheerily past him till he saw the village before him
and broke into song; but as soon as he was out of sight
of the house he turned and stooping behind a fold of
the ground ran back to the desolate wood. There he
waited watching the evil house, just too far to hear
voices. The sun was low already. He chose the window at which he meant to eavesdrop, a little barred
one at the back, close to the ground. And then the pi-
geons came in; for a great distance there was no other
wood, so numbers shelter there, though the clump is
small and of so evil a look (if they notice that); the
first one frightened Amuel, he felt that it might be a
spirit escaped from torture in some dim parlour of the
house that he watched, his nerves were strained and
he feared foolish fears. Then he grew used to them
and the sun set then and the aspect of everything altered and he felt strange fears again. Behind him was
a hollow in the wold, he watched it darkening; and

before him he saw the house through the trunks of the trees. He waited for them to light their lamps so that they could not see, when he would steal up softly and crouch by the little back window. But though every bird was home, though the night grew chilly as tombs, though a star was out, still there shone no yellow light from any window. Amuel waited and shuddered. He did not dare to move till they lit their lamps, they might be watching. The damp and the cold so strangely affected him that autumn evening and the remnants of sunset, the stars and the wold and the whole vault of the sky seemed like a hall that they had prepared for Fear. He began to feel a dread of prodigious things, and still no light shone in the evil house. It grew so dark that he decided to move and make his way to the window in spite of the stillness and though the house was dark. He rose and while standing arrested by pains that cramped his limbs, he heard the door swing open on the far side of the house. He had just time to hide behind the trunk of a pine when the three grim men approached him and the woman hobbled behind. Right to the ominous clump of trees they came as though they loved their blackness, passed through within a yard or two of the postman and squatted down on their haunches in a ring in the hollow behind the trees. They lit a fire in the hollow and laid a kid on the fire and by the light of it Amuel saw brought forth from an untanned pouch the letter that came from China. The elder opened it with his gristly hand and intoning words that Amuel did not know, drew out from it a green powder and sprinkled it on the fire. At once a flame arose and a wonderful savour, the flames rose higher and flickered turning the trees all green; and Amuel saw the gods coming to snuff the savour. While the three grim men prostrated themselves by their fire, and the horrible woman that was the spouse of one, he saw the gods coming gauntly over the wold, beheld the gods of Old England hungrily snuffing the savour, Odin, Balder, and Thor, the gods of the ancient people, beheld them eye to eye clear and close in the twilight, and the office of post-man fell vacant in Otford-under-the-Wold.

In the harbour, between the liner and the palms, as the huge ship's passengers came up from dinner, at moonrise, each in his canoe, Ali Kareeb Ahash and Boob Aheera passed within knife thrust.

So urgent was the purpose of Ali Kareeb Ahash that he did not lean over as his enemy slid by, did not tarry then to settle that long account; but that Boob Aheera made no attempt to reach him was a source of wonder to Ali. He pondered it till the liner's electric lights shone far away behind him with one blaze and the canoe was near to his destination, and pondered it in vain, for all that the eastern subtlety of his mind was able to tell him clearly was that it was not like Boob Aheera to pass him like that.

That Boob Aheera could have dared to lay such a cause as his before the Diamond Idol Ali had not conceived, yet as he drew near to the golden shrine in the palms, that none that come by the great ships ever found, he began to see more clearly in his mind that this was where Boob had gone on that hot night. And when he beached his canoe his fears departed, giving place to the resignation with which he always viewed Destiny; for there on the white sea sand were the tracks of another canoe, the edges all fresh and ragged. Boob Aheera had been before him. Ali did not blame himself for being late, the thing had been planned before the beginning of time, by gods that knew their business; only his hate of Boob Aheera increased, his enemy against whom he had come to pray. And the more his hate increased the more clearly he saw him, until nothing else could be seen by the eye of his mind but the dark lean figure, the little lean legs, the grey beard and neat loin-cloth of Boob Aheera, his enemy.

That the Diamond Idol should have granted the prayers of such a one he did not as yet imagine, he hated him merely for his presumptuousness in approaching the shrine at all, for approaching it before him whose cause was righteous, for many an old past wrong, but most of all for the expression of his face and the general look of the man as he has swept by in his canoe with his double paddle going in the moonlight.

Ali pushed through the steaming vegetation. The place smelt of orchids. There is no track to the shrine though many go. If there were a track the white man would one day find it, and parties would row to see it whenever a liner came in; and photographs would appear in weekly papers with accounts of it underneath by men who had never left London, and all the mystery would be gone away and there would be nothing novel in this story.

Ali had scarcely gone a hundred yards through cactus and creeper underneath the palms when he came to the golden shrine that nothing guards except the deeps of the forest, and found the Diamond Idol. The Diamond Idol is five inches high and its base a good inch square, and it has a greater lustre than those diamonds that Mr. Moses bought last year for his wife, when he offered her an earldom or the diamonds, and Jael his wife had answered, "Buy the diamonds and be just plain Mr. Fortescue."

Purer than those was its luster and carved as they carve not in Europe, and the men thereby are poor and held to be fearless—yet they do not sell that idol. And I may say here that if any one of my readers should ever come by ship to the winding harbour where the forts of the Portuguese crumble in infinite greenery, where the baobab stands like a corpse here and there in the palms, if he goes ashore where no one has any business to go, and where no one so far as I know has gone from a liner before (though it's little more than a mile or so from the pier), and if he finds a golden shrine, which is near enough to the shore, and a five-inch diamond in it carved in the shape of a god, it is better to leave it alone and get back safe to the ship than to sell that diamond idol for any price in the world.

Ali Kareeb Ahash went into the golden shrine, and when he raised his head from the seven obeisances that are the due of the idol, behold! it glowed with such a lustre as only it wears after answering recent prayer. No native of those parts mistakes the tone of the idol, they know its varying shades as a tracker knows blood; the moon was streaming in through the open door and Ali saw it clearly.

No one had been that night but Boob Aheera.

The fury of Ali rose and surged to his heart, he clutched his knife till the hilt of it bruised his hand, yet he did not utter the prayer that he had made ready about Boob Aheera's liver, for he saw that Boob Aheera's prayers were acceptable to the idol and knew that divine protection was over his enemy.

What Boob Aheera's prayer was he did not know, but he went back to the beach as fast as one can go through cacti and creepers that climb to the tops of the palms; and as fast as his canoe could carry him he went down the winding harbour, till the liner shone beside him as he passed, and he heard the sound of its band rise up and die, and he landed and came that night into Boob Aheera's hut. And there he offered himself as his enemy's slave, and Boob Aheera's slave he is to this day, and his master has protection from the idol. And Ali rows to the liners and goes on board to sell rubies made of glass, and thin suits for the tropics and ivory napkin rings, and Manchester kimonos, and little lovely shells; and the passengers abuse him because of his prices; and yet they should not, for all the money cheated by Ali Kareeb Ahash goes to Boob Aheera, his master.

It was dead of night and midwinter. A frightful wind was bringing sleet from the East. The long sere grasses were wailing. Two specks of light appeared on the desolate plain; a man in a hansom cab was driving alone in North China.

Alone with the driver and the dejected horse. The driver wore a good waterproof cape, and of course an oiled silk hat, but the man in the cab wore nothing but evening dress. He did not have the glass door down because the horse fell so frequently, the sleet had put his cigar out and it was too cold to sleep; the two lamps flared in the wind. By the uncertain light of a candle lamp that flickered inside the cab, a Manchu shepherd that saw the vehicle pass, where he watched his sheep on the plain in fear of the wolves, for the first time saw evening dress. And though he saw if dimly, and what he saw was wet, it was like a backward glance of a thousand years, for as his civilization is so much older than ours they have presumably passed through all that kind of thing.

He watched it stoically, not wondering at a new thing, if indeed it be new to China, meditated on it awhile in a manner strange to us, and when he had added to his philosophy what little could be derived from the sight of this hansom cab, returned to his contemplation of that night's chances of wolves and to such occasional thoughts as he drew at times for his comfort out of the legends of China, that have been preserved for such uses. And on such a night their comfort was greatly needed. He thought of the legend of a dragon-lady, more fair than the flowers are, without an equal amongst daughters of men, humanly lovely to look on although her sire was a dragon, yet one who traced his descent from gods of the elder days, and so it was that she went in all her ways divine, like the earliest ones of her race, who were holier than the emperor.

She had come down one day out of her little land, a grassy valley hidden amongst the mountains; by the way of the mountain passes she came down, and the rocks of the rugged pass rang like little bells about her, as her bare feet went by, like silver bells to please her; and the sound was like the sound of the dromedaries of a prince when they come home at evening—their silver bells are ringing and the village-folk are glad. She had come down to pick the enchanted poppy that grew, and grows to this day—if only men might find it—in a field at the feet of the mountains; if one should pick it happiness would come to all yellow men, victory without fighting, good wages, and ceaseless ease. She came down all fair from the mountains; and as the legend pleasantly passed through his mind in the bitterest hour of the night, which comes before dawn, two lights appeared and another hansom went by.

The man in the second cab was dressed the same as the first, he was wetter than the first, for the sleet had fallen all night, but evening dress is evening dress all the world over. The driver wore the same oiled hat, the same waterproof cape as the other. And when the cab had passed the darkness swirled back where the two small lamps had been, and the slush poured into the wheel-tracks and nothing remained but the speculations of the shepherd to tell that a hansom cab had been in that part of China; presently even these ceased, and he was back with the early legends again in contemplation of serener things.

And the storm and the cold and the darkness made one last effort, and shook the bones of that shepherd, and rattled the teeth in the head that mused on the flowery fables, and suddenly it was morning. You saw the outlines of the sheep all of a sudden, the shepherd counted them, no wolf had come, you could see them all quite clearly. And in the pale light of the earliest morning the third hansom appeared, with its lamps still burning, looking ridiculous in the daylight. They came out of the East with the sleet and were all going due westwards, and the occupant of the third cab also wore evening dress.

Calmly that Manchu shepherd, without curiosity, still less with wonder, but as one who would see whatever life has to show him, stood for four hours to see if another would come. The sleet and the East wind continued. And at the end of four hours another came. The driver was urging it on as fast as he could, as though he were making the most of the daylight, his cabby's cape was flapping wildly about him; inside the cab a man in evening dress was being jolted up and down by the unevenness of the plain.

This was of course that famous race from Pittsburg to Piccadilly, going round by the long way, that started one night after dinner from Mr. Flagdrop's house, and was won by Mr. Kagg, driving the Honourable Alfred

Fortescue, whose father it will be remembered was Hagar Dermstein, and became (by Letters Patent) Sir Edgar Fortescue, and finally Lord St. George.

The Manchu shepherd stood there till evening, and when he saw that no more cabs would come, turned homeward in search of food.

And the rice prepared for him was hot and good, all the more after the bitter coldness of that sleet. And when he had consumed it her perused his experience, turning over again in his mind each detail of the cabs he had seen; and from that his thoughts slipped calmly to the glorious history of China, going back to the indecorous times before calmness came, and beyond those times to the happy days of the earth when the gods and dragons were here and China was young; and lighting his opium pipe and casting his thoughts easily forward he looked to the time when the dragons shall come again.

And for a long while then his mind reposed itself in such a dignified calm that no thought stirred there at all, from which when he was aroused he cast off his lethargy as a man emerges from the baths, refreshed, cleansed and contented, and put away from his musings the things he had seen on the plain as being evil and of the nature of dreams, or futile illusion, the results of activity which troubleth calm. And then he turned his mind toward the shape of God, the One, the Ineffable, who sits by the lotus lily, whose shape is the shape of peace, and denieth activity, and went out his thanks to him that he had cast all bad customs westward out of China as a woman throws household dirt out of her basket far out into neighbouring gardens.

From thankfulness he turned to calm again, and out of calm to sleep.

On one of those unattained, and unattainable pinnacles that are known as the Bleaks of Eerie, an eagle was looking East with a hopeful presage of blood.

For he knew, and rejoiced in the knowledge, that eastward over the dells the dwarfs were risen in Ulk, and gone to war with the demi-gods.

The demi-gods are they that were born of earthly women, but their sires are the elder gods who walked of old among men. Disguised they would go through the villages sometimes in summer evenings, cloaked and unknown of men; but the younger maidens knew them and always ran to them singing, for all that their elders said: in evenings long ago they had danced to the woods of the oak-trees. Their children dwelt out-of-doors beyond the dells of the bracken, in the cool and heathery lands, and were now at war with the dwarfs.

Dour and grim were the demi-gods and had the faults of both parents, and would not mix with men but claimed the right of their fathers, and would not play human games but forever were prophesying, and yet were more frivolous than their mothers were, whom the fairies had long since buried in wild wood gardens with more than human rites.

And being irked at their lack of rights and ill content with the land, and having no power at all over the wind and snow, and caring little for the powers they had, the demi-gods became idle, greasy, and slow; and the contemptuous dwarfs despised them ever.

The dwarfs were contemptuous of all things savouring of heaven, and of everything that was even partly divine. They were, so it has been said, of the seed of man; but, being squat and hairy like to the beasts; they praised all beastly things, and bestiality was shown reverence among them, so far as reverence was theirs to show. So most of all they despised the discontent of the demi-gods, who dreamed of the courts of heaven and power over wind and snow; for what better, said the dwarfs, could demi-gods do than nose in the earth for roots and cover their faces with mire, and run with the cheerful goats and be even as they?

Now in their idleness caused by their discontent, the seed of the gods and the maidens grew more discontented still, and only spake of or cared for heavenly things; until the contempt of the dwarfs, who heard of all these doings, was bridled no longer and it must needs be war. They burned spice, dipped in blood and dried, before the chief of their witches, sharpening their axes, and made war on the demi-gods.

They passed by night over the Oolnar Mountains, each dwarf with his good axe, the old flint war-axe of his fathers, a night when no moon shone, and they went unshod, and swiftly, to come on the demi-gods in the darkness beyond the dells of Ulk, lying fat and idle and contemptible.

And before it was light they found the heathery lands, and the demi-gods lying lazy all over the side of a hill. The dwarfs stole towards them warily in the darkness.

Now the art that the gods love most is the art of war: and when the seed of the gods and those nimble maidens awoke and found it was war it was almost as much to them as the godlike pursuits of heaven, enjoyed in the marble courts; or power over wind and snow. They all drew out at once their swords of tempered bronze, cast down to them centuries since on stormy nights when their fathers, drew them and faced the dwarfs, and casting their idleness from them, fell on them, sword to axe. And the dwarfs fought hard that night, and bruised the demi-gods sorely, hacking with those huge axes that had not spared the oaks. Yet for all the weight of their blows and the cunning of their adventure, one point they had overlooked: *the demi-gods were immortal.*

As the fight rolled on towards morning the fighters were fewer and fewer, yet for all the blows of the dwarfs men fell upon one side only.

Dawn came and the demi-gods were fighting against no more than six, and the hour that follows dawn, and the last of the dwarfs was gone.

And when the light was clear on that peak of the Bleaks of Eerie the eagle left his crag and flew grimly East, and found it was as he had hoped in the matter of blood.

But the demi-gods lay down in their heathery lands, for once content though so far from the courts of heaven, and even half forgot their heavenly rights, and sighed no more for power over wind and snow.

M eoul Ki Ning was on his way with a lily from the lotus ponds of Esh to offer it to the Goddess of Abundance in her temple Aoul Keroon. And on the road from the pond to the little hill and the temple Aoul Keroon, Ap Ariph, his enemy, shot him with an arrow from a bow that he had made out of bamboo, and took his pretty lily up the hill and offered it to the Goddess of Abundance in her temple Aoul Keroon. And the Goddess was pleased with the gift, as all women are, and sent pleasant dreams to Ap Ariph for seven nights straight from the moon.

And on the seventh night the gods held conclave together, on the cloudy peaks they held it, above Narn, Ktoon, and Pti. So high their peak arises that no man heard their voices. They spake on that cloudy mountain (not the highest hamlet heard them). "What doth the Goddess of Abundance," (but naming her Lling, as they name her), "what doth she sending sweet dreams for seven nights to Ap Ariph?"

And the gods sent for their seer who is all eyes and feet, running to and fro on the Earth, observing the ways of men, seeing even their littlest doings, never deeming a doing too little, but knowing the web of the gods is woven of littlest things. He it is that sees the cat in the garden of parakeets, the thief in the upper chamber, the sin of the child with the honey, the women talking indoors and the small hut's innermost things. Standing before the gods he told them the case of Ap Ariph and the wrongs of Meoul Ki Ning and the rape of the lotus lily; he told of the cutting and making of Ap Ariph's bamboo bow, of the shooting of Meoul Ki Ning, and of how the arrow hit him, and the smile on the face of Lling when she came by the lotus bloom.

And the gods were wroth with Ap Ariph and swore to avenge Ki Ning.

And the ancient one of the gods, he that is older than Earth, called up the thunder at once, and raised his arms and cried out on the gods' high windy mountain, and prophesied on those rocks with runes that were older than speech, and sang in his wrath old songs that he had learned in storm from the sea, when only that peak of the gods in the whole of the earth was dry; and he swore that Ap Ariph should die that night, and the thunder raged about him, and the tears of Lling were vain.

The lightning stroke of the gods leaping earthward seeking Ap Ariph passed near to his house but missed him. A certain vagabond was down from the hills, singing songs in the street near by the house of Ap Ariph, songs of a former folk that dwelt once, they say, in those valleys, and begging for rice and curds; it was him the lightning hit.

And the gods were satisfied, and their wrath abated, and their thunder rolled away and the great black clouds dissolved, and the ancient one of the gods went back to his age-old sleep, and morning came, and the birds and the light shone on the mountain, and the peak stood clear to see, the serene home of the gods.

There was once a man who sought a boon of the gods. For peace was over the world and all things savoured of sameness, and the man was weary at heart and sighed for the tents and the warfields. Therefore he sought a boon of the ancient gods. And appearing before them he said to them, "Ancient gods; there is peace in the land where I dwell, and indeed to the uttermost parts, and we are full weary of peace. O ancient gods, grant us war!"

And the ancient gods made him a war.

And the man went forth with his sword, and behold it was even war. And the man remembered the little things that he knew, and thought of the quiet days that there used to be, and at night on the hard ground dreamed of the things of peace. And dearer and dearer grew the wonted things, the dull but easeful things of the days of peace, and remembering these he began to regret the war, and sought once more a boon of the ancient gods, and appearing before them he said: "O ancient gods, indeed but a man loves best the days of peace. Therefore take back your war and give us peace, for indeed of all your blessedness peace is best."

And the man returned again to the haunts of peace.

But in a while the man grew weary of peace, of the things that he used to know, and the savour of sameness again; and sighing again for the tents, and appearing once more to the gods, he said to them: "Ancient gods; we do not love your peace, for indeed the days are dull, and a man is best at war."

And the gods made him a war.

And there were drums again, the smoke of campfires again, wind in the waste again, the sound of horses of war, burning cities again, and the things that wanderers know; and the thoughts of that man went home to the ways of peace; moss upon lawns again, light in old spires again, sun upon gardens again, flowers in pleasant woods and sleep and the paths of peace.

And once more the man appeared to the ancient gods and sought from them one more boon, and said to them: "Ancient gods; indeed but the world and we are a-weary of war and long for the ancient ways and the paths of peace."

So the gods took back their war and gave him peace.

But the man took counsel one day and communed long with himself and said to himself: "Behold, the wishes I wish, which the gods grant, are not to be much desired; and if the gods should one day grant a wish and never revoke it, which is a way of the gods, I should be sorely tried because of my wish; my wishes are dangerous wishes and not to be desired."

And therefore he wrote an anonymous letter to the gods, writing: "O ancient gods; this man that hath four times troubled you with his wishes, wishing for peace and war, is a man that hath no reverence for the gods, speaking ill of them on days when they do not hear, and speaking well of them on holy days and at the appointed hours when the gods are hearkening to prayer. Therefore grant no more wishes to this impious man."

And the days of peace wore on and there arose again from the earth, like mist in the autumn from the fields that generations have ploughed, the savour of sameness again. And the man went forth one morning and appeared once more to the gods, and cried: "O ancient gods; give us but one war again, for I would be back to the camps and debateable borders of lands."

And the gods said: "We hear not well of your way of life, yea ill things have come to our hearing, so that we grant no more the wishes you wish."

THE SACK OF EMERALDS

One bad October night in the high wolds beyond Wiltshire, with a north wind chaunting of winter, with the old leaves letting go their hold one by one from branches and dropping down to decay, with a mournful sound of owls, and in fearsome loneliness, there trudged in broken boots and in wet and windy rags an old man, stooping low under a sack of emeralds. It were easy to see had you been travelling late on that inauspicious night, that the burden of the sack was far too great for the poor old man that bore it. And had you flashed a lantern in his face there was a look there of hopelessness and fatigue that would have told you it was no wish of his that kept him tottering on under that bloated sack.

When the menacing look of the night and its cheerless sounds, and the cold, and the weight of the sack, had all but brought him to the door of death, and he had dropped his sack onto the road and was dragging it on behind him, just as he felt that his final hour was come, and come (which was worse) as he held the accursed sack, just then he saw the bulk and the black shape of the Sign of the Lost Shepherd loom up by the ragged way. He opened the door and staggered into the light and sank on a bench with his huge sack beside him.

All this you had seen had you been on that lonely road, so late on those bitter wolds, with their outlines vast and mournful in the dark, and their little clumps of trees sad with October. But neither you nor I were out that night. I did not see the poor old man and his sack until he sank down all of a heap in the lighted inn.

And Yon the blacksmith was there; and the carpenter, Willie Losh; and Jackers, the postman's son. And they gave him a glass of beer. And the old man drank it up, still hugging his emeralds.

And at last they asked him what he had in his sack, the question he clearly dreaded; and he only clasped yet tighter the sodden sack and mumbled he had potatoes.

"Potatoes," said Yon the blacksmith.

"Potatoes," said Willie Losh.

And when he heard the doubt that was in their voices the old man shivered and moaned.

"Potatoes, did you say?" said the postman's son. And they all three rose and tried to peer at the sack that the rain-soaked wayfarer so zealously sheltered.

And from the old man's fierceness I had said that, had it not been for that foul night on the roads and the weight he had carried so far and the fearful winds of October, he had fought with the blacksmith, the carpenter and the postman's son, all three, till he beat them away from his sack. And weary and wet as he was he fought them hard.

I should no doubt have interfered; and yet the three men meant no harm to the wayfarer, but resented the reticence that he displayed to them though they had given him beer; it was to them as though a master key had failed to open a cupboard. And, as for me, curiosity held me down to my chair and forbade me to interfere on behalf of the sack; for the old man's furtive ways, and the night out of which he came, and the hour of his coming, and the look of his sack, all made me long as much to know what he had, as even the blacksmith, the carpenter and the postman's son.

And then they found the emeralds. They were all bigger than hazel nuts, hundreds and hundreds of them: and the old man screamed.

"Come, come, we're not thieves," said the blacksmith.

"We're not thieves," said the carpenter.

"We're not thieves," said the postman's son.

And with awful fear on his face the wayfarer closed his sack, whimpering over his emeralds and furtively glancing round as though the loss of his secret were and utterly deadly thing. And then they asked him to give them just one each, just one huge emerald each, because they had given him a glass of beer. Then to see the wayfarer shrink against his sack and guard it with clutching fingers one would have said that he was a selfish man, were it not for the terror that was freezing his face. I have seen men look sheer at Death with far less fear.

And they took their emerald all three, one enormous emerald each, while the old man hopelessly struggled till he saw his three emeralds go, and fell to the floor and wept, a pitiable, sodden heap.

And about that time I began to hear far off down the windy road, by which that sack had come, faintly at first and slowly louder and louder, the click clack clop of a lame horse coming nearer. Click clack clop and a loose shoe rattling, the sound of a horse too weary to be out upon such a night, too lame to be out at all.

Click clack clop. And all of a sudden the old wayfarer heard it; heard it above the sound of his won sobbing, and at once went white to the lips. Such sudden fear as blanched him in a moment struck right to the hearts of all there. They muttered to him that it was only their play, they hastily whispered excuses, they asked him what was wrong, but seemed scarcely to hope for an answer, nor did he speak, but sat with a frozen stare, all at once dry-eyed, a monument to terror.

Nearer and nearer came the click clack clop.

And when I saw the expression of that man's face and how its horror deepened as the ominous sound drew nearer, then I knew that something was wrong. And looking for the last time upon all four I saw the wayfarer horror-struck by his sack and the other three crowding round to put their huge emeralds back then, even on such a night, I slipped away from the inn.

Outside the bitter wind roared in my ears, and close in the darkness the horse went click clack clop.

And as soon as my eyes could see at all in the night I saw a man in a huge hat looped up in front, wearing a sword in a scabbard shabby and huge, and looking blacker than the darkness, riding on a lean horse slowly up to the inn. Whether his were the emeralds, or who he was, or why he rode a lame horse on such a night, I did not stop to discover, but went at once from the inn as he strode in his great black riding coat up to the door.

And that was the last that was ever seen of the wayfarer; the blacksmith, the carpenter or the postman's son.

THE OLD BROWN COAT

My friend, Mr. Douglas Ainslie, tells me that Sir James Barrie once told him this story. The story, or rather the fragment, was as follows.

A man strolling into an auction somewhere abroad, I think it must have been France, for they bid in francs, found they were selling old clothes. And following some idle whim he soon found himself bidding for an old coat. A man bid against him, he bid against the man. Up and up went the price till the old coat was knocked down to him for twenty pounds. As he went away with the coat he saw the other bidder looking at him with an expression of fury.

That's as far as the story goes. But how, Mr. Ainslie asked me, did the matter develop, and why that furious look? I at once made enquiries at a reliable source and have ascertained that the man's name was Peters, who thus oddly purchased a coat, and that he took it to the Rue de Rivoli, to a hotel where he lodged, from the little low, dark auction room by the Seine in which he concluded the bargain. There he examined it, off and on, all day and much of the next morning, a light brown overcoat with tails, without discovering any excuse, far less a reason, for having spent twenty pounds on so worn a thing. And late next morning to his sitting room looking out on the Gardens of the Tuileries the man with the furious look was ushered in.

Grim he stood, silent and angry, till the guiding waiter went. Not till then did he speak, and his words came clear and brief, welling up from deep emotions.

"How did you dare to bid against me?"

His name was Santiago. And for many moments Peters found no excuse to offer, no apology, nothing in extenuation. Lamely at last, weakly, knowing his argument to be of no avail, he muttered something to the intent that Mr. Santiago could have outbid him.

"No," said the stranger. "We don't want all the town in this. This is a matter between you and me." He paused, then added in his fierce, curt way: "A thousand pounds, no more."

Almost dumbly Peters accepted the offer and, pocketing the thousand pounds that was paid him, and apologizing for the inconvenience he had unwittingly caused, tried to show the stranger out. But Santiago strode swiftly on before him, taking the coat, and was gone.

There followed between Peters and his second thoughts another long afternoon of bitter reproaches. Why ever had he let go so thoughtlessly of a garment that so easily fetched a thousand pounds? And the more he brooded on this the more clearly did he perceive that he had lost an unusual opportunity of a first class investment of a speculative kind. He knew men perhaps better than he knew materials; and, though he could not see in that old brown coat the value of so much as a thousand pounds, he saw far more than that in the man's eager need for it. An afternoon of brooding over lost opportunities led to a night of remorse, and scarcely had day dawned when he ran to his sitting-room to see if he still had safe the card of Santiago. And there was the neat and perfumed *carte de visite* with Santiago's Parisian address in the corner.

That morning he sought him out, and found Santiago seated at a table with chemicals and magnifying glasses beside him examining, as it lay spread wide before him, the old brown coat. And Peters fancied he wore a puzzled air.

They came at once to business. Peters was rich and asked Santiago to name his price, and that small dark man admitted financial straits, and so was willing to sell for thirty thousand pounds. A little bargaining followed, the price came down and the old brown coat changed hands once more, for twenty thousand pounds.

Let any who may be inclined to doubt my story understand that in the City, as any respectable company promoter will tell them, twenty thousand pounds is invested almost daily with less return for it than an old tail coat. And, whatever doubts Mr. Peters felt that day about the wisdom of his investment, there before him lay that tangible return, that something that may be actually fingered and seen, which is so often denied to the investor in gold mines and other Selected Investments. Yet as the days wore on and the old coat grew no younger, nor any more wonderful, nor the least useful, but more and more like an ordinary old coat, Peters began once more to doubt his astuteness. Before the week was out his doubts had grown acute. And then one morning, Santiago returned. A man, he said, had just arrived from Spain, a friend unexpected all of a sudden in Paris, from whom he might borrow money: and would Peters resell the coat for thirty thousand pounds?

It was then that Peters, seeing his opportunity, cast aside the pretence that he had maintained for so long of knowing something about the mysterious coat, and demanded to know its properties. Santiago swore that he knew not, and repeatedly swore the same by many sacred names; but when Peters as often threatened not to sell, Santiago at last drew out a thin cigar and, lighting it and settling himself in a chair, told all he knew of the coat.

He had been on its tracks for weeks with suspicions growing all the time that it was no ordinary coat, and at last he had run it to earth in that auction room but would not bid for it more than twenty pounds for fear of letting every one into the secret. What the secret was he swore he did not know, but this much he knew all along, that the weight of the coat was absolutely nothing; and he had discovered by testing it with acids that the brown stuff of which the coat was made was neither cloth nor silk nor any known material, and would neither burn nor tear. He believed it to be some undiscovered element. And the properties of the coat which he was convinced were marvellous he felt sure of discovering within another week by means of experiments with his chemicals. Again he offered thirty thousand pounds, to be paid within two or three days if all went well. And then they started haggling together as business men will.

And all the morning went by over the gardens of the Tuileries and the afternoons came on, and only by two o'clock they arrived at an understanding, on a basis, as they called it, of thirty thousand guineas. And the old tail coat was brought out and spread on the table, and they examined it together and chatted about its properties, all the more friendly for their strenuous argument. And Santiago was rising up to go, and Peters pleasantly holding out his hand, when a step was heard on the stair. It echoed up to the room, the door opened. And an elderly labouring man came stumping in. He walked with difficulty, almost like a bather who has been swimming and floating all morning and misses the buoyancy of the water when he has come to land. He stumped up to the table without speaking and there at once caught sight of the old brown coat.

"Why," he said, "that be my old coat."

And without another word he put it on. In the fierce glare of his eyes as he fitted on that coat, carefully fastening the buttons, buttoning up the flap of a pocket here, unbuttoning one there, neither Peters nor Santiago found a word to say. They sat there wondering how they had dared to bid for that brown tail coat, how they had dared to buy it, even to touch it, they sat there silent without a single excuse. And with no word more the old labourer stumped across the room, opened wide the double window that looked on the Tuileries gardens and, flashing back over his shoulder one look that was full of scorn, stumped away up through the air at an angle of forty degrees.

Peters and Santiago saw him bear to his left from the window; passing diagonally over the Rue de Rivoli and over a corner of the Tuileries gardens; they saw him clear the Louvre, and thence they dumbly watched him still slanting upwards, stepping out with a firmer and more confident stride as he dwindled and dwindled away with his old brown coat.

Neither spoke till he was no more than a speck in the sky far away over Paris going South Eastwards.

"Well I am blowed," said Peters.

But Santiago sadly shook his head. "I knew it was a good coat," he said. "I *knew* it was a good coat."

It is told in the Archive of the Older Mysteries of China that one of the house of Tlang was cunning with sharpened iron and went to the green jade mountains and carved a green jade god. And this was in the cycle of the Dragon, the seventy-eighth year.

And for nearly a hundred years men doubted the green jade god, and then they worshipped him for a thousand years; and after that they doubted him again, and the green jade god made a miracle and whelmed the green jade mountains, sinking them down one evening at sunset into the earth so that there is only a marsh where the green jade mountains were. And the marsh is full of the lotus.

By the side of this lotus marsh, just as it glitters at evening, walks Li La Ting, the Chinese girl, to bring the cows home; she goes behind them singing of the river Lo Lang Ho. And thus she sings of the river, even of Lo Lang Ho: she sings that he is indeed of all rivers the greatest, born of more ancient mountains than even the wise men know, swifter than hares, more deep than the sea, the master of other rivers perfumed even as roses and fairer than the sapphires around the neck of a prince. And then she would pray to the river Lo Lang Ho, master of rivers and rival of the heaven at dawn, to bring her down in a boat of light bamboo a lover rowing out of the inner land in a garment of yellow silk with turquoises at his waist, young and merry and idle, with a face as yellow as gold and a ruby in his cap with lanterns shining at dusk.

Thus she would pray of an evening to the river Lo Lang Ho as she went behind the cows at the edge of the lotus marshes and the green jade god under the lotus marshes was jealous of the lover that the maiden Li La Ting would pray for of an evening to the river Lo Lang Ho, and he cursed the river after the manner of gods and turned it into a narrow and evil smelling stream.

And all this happened a thousand years ago, and Lo Lang Ho is but a reproach among travelers and the story of that great river is forgotten, and what became of the maiden no tale saith though all men think she became a goddess of jade to sit and smile at a lotus on a lotus carven of stone by the side of the green jade god far under the marshes upon the peaks of the mountains, but women know that her ghost still haunts the lotus marshes on glittering evenings, singing of Lo Lang Ho.

P ast the upper corner of a precipice the moon rode into view. Night had for some while now hooded the marvelous city. They had planned it to be symmetrical, its maps were orderly, near; in two dimensions, that is length and breadth, its streets met and crossed each other with regular exactitude, with all the dullness of the science of man. The city had laughed as it were and shaken itself free and in the third dimension had soared away to consort with all the careless, irregular things that know not man for their master.

Yet even there, even at those altitudes, man had still clung to his symmetry, still claimed that these mountains were houses; in orderly rows the thousand windows stood watching each other precisely, all orderly, all alike, lest any should guess by day that there might be mystery here. So they stood in the daylight. The sun set, still they were orderly, as scientific and regular as the labour of only man and the bees. The mists darken at evening. And first the Woolworth Building goes away, sheer home and away from any allegiance to man, to take his place among mountains; for I saw him stand with the lower slopes invisible in the gloaming, while only his pinnacles showed up in the clearer sky. Thus only mountains stand.

Still all the windows of the other buildings stood in their regular rows—all side by side in silence, not yet changed, as though waiting one furtive moment to step from the schemes of man, to slip back to mystery and romance again as cats do when they steal on velvet feet away from familiar hearths in the dark of the moon.

Night fell, and the moment came. Someone lit a window, far up another shone with its orange glow. Window by window, and yet not nearly all. Surely if modern man with his clever schemes held any sway here still he would have turned one switch and lit them all together; but we are back with the older man of whom far songs tell, he whose spirit is kin to strange romances and mountains. One by one the windows shine from the precipices; some twinkle, some are dark; man's orderly schemes have gone, and we are amongst vast heights lit by inscrutable beacons.

I have seen such cities before, and I have told of them in *The Book of Wonder*.

Here in New York a poet met a welcome.

Publisher's Note

Beyond the fields we know, in the Lands of Dream, lies the Valley of the Yann where the mighty river of that name, rising in the Hills of Hap, idleing its way by massive dream-evoking amethyst cliffs, orchid-laden forests, and ancient mysterious cities, comes to the Gates of Yann and passes to the sea.

Some years since a poet visiting that land voyaged down the Yann on a trading bark named the *Bird of the River* and returning safe to Ireland, set down in a tale that is called *Idle Days on the Yann,* the wonders of that voyage. Now the tale being one of marvellous beauty, found its way into a volume we call *A Dreamer's Tales* where it may be found to this day with other wondrous tales of that same poet.

As the days went by the lure of the river and pleasant memories of his shipmates bore in with a constant urge on the soul of the poet that he might once more journey Beyond the Fields We Know and come to the floor of Yann; and one day it fell out that turning into Go-by

Street that leads up from the Embankment toward the Strand and which you and I always do go by and perhaps never see in passing, he found the door which one enters on the way to the Land of Dream.

Twice of late has Lord Dunsany entered that door in Go-by Street and returned to the Valley of the Yann and each time come back with a tale; one, of his search for the *Bird of the River,* the other of the mighty hunter who avenged the destruction of Perdondaris, where on his earlier voyage the captain tied up his ship and traded within the city. That all may be clear to those who read these new tales and to whom no report has previously come Beyond the Fields We Know the publishers reprint in this volume *Idle Days on the Yann.*

First Tale: Idle Days on the Yann

So I came down through the wood to the bank of Yann and found, as had been prophesied, the ship *Bird of the River* about to loose her cable.

The captain sate cross-legged upon the white deck with his scimitar lying beside him in its jewelled scabbard, and the sailors toiled to spread the nimble sails to bring the ship into the central stream of Yann, and all the while sang ancient soothing songs. And the wind of the evening descending cool from the snowfields of some mountainous abode of distant gods came suddenly, like glad tidings to an anxious city, into the wing-like sails.

And so we came into the central stream, whereat the sailors lowered the greater sails. But I had gone to bow before the captain, and to inquire concerning the miracles, and appearances among men, of the most holy gods of whatever land he had come from. And the captain answered that he came from fair Belzoond, and worshipped gods that were the least and humblest, who seldom sent the famine or the thunder, and were easily appeased with little battles. And I told how I came from Ireland, which is of Europe, whereat the captain and all the sailors laughed, for they said, "There are no such places in all the land of dreams." When they had ceased to mock me, I explained that my fancy mostly dwelt in the desert of Cuppar-Nombo, about a beautiful city called Golthoth the Damned, which was sentinelled all round by wolves and their shadows, and had been utterly desolate for years and years, because of a curse which the gods once spoke in anger and could never since recall. And sometimes my dreams took me as far as Pungar Vees, the red walled city where the fountains are, which trades with the Isles and Thul. When I said this they complimented me upon the abode of my fancy, saying that, though they had never seen these cities, such places might well be imagined. For the rest of that evening I bargained with the captain over the sum that I should pay him for my fare if God and the tide of Yann should bring us safely as far as the cliffs by the sea, which are named Bar-Wul-Yann, the Gate of Yann.

And now the sun had set, and all the colours of the world and heaven had held a festival with him, and slipped one by one away before the imminent approach of night. The parrots had all flown home to the jungle on either bank, the monkeys in rows in safety on high branches of the trees were silent and asleep, the fireflies in the deeps of the forest were going up and down, and the great stars came gleaming out to look on the face of Yann. Then the sailors lighted lanterns and hung them round the ship, and the light flashed out on a sudden and dazzled Yann, and the ducks that fed along his marshy banks all suddenly arose, and made wide circles in the upper air, and saw the distant reaches of the Yann and the white mist that softly cloaked the jungle, before they returned again into their marshes.

And then the sailors knelt on the decks and prayed, not all together, but five or six at a time. Side by side there kneeled down together five or six, for there only prayed at the same time men of different faiths, so that no god should hear two men praying to him at once. As soon as any one had finished his prayer, another of the same faith would take his place. Thus knelt the row of five or six with bended heads under the fluttering sail, while the central stream of the River Yann took them on towards the sea, and their prayers rose up from among the lanterns and went towards the stars. And behind them in the after end of the ship the helmsman prayed aloud the helmsman's prayer, which is prayed by all who follow his trade upon the River Yann, of whatever faith they be. And the captain prayed to his little lesser gods, to the gods that bless Belzoond.

And I too felt that I would pray. Yet I liked not to pray to a jealous God there where the frail affectionate gods whom the heathen love were being humbly invoked; so I bethought me, instead, of Sheol Nugganoth, whom the men of the jungle have long since deserted, who is now unworshipped and alone; and to him I prayed.

And upon us praying the night came suddenly down, as it comes upon all men who pray at evening and upon all men who do not; yet our prayers comforted our own souls when we thought of the Great Night to come.

And so Yann bore us magnificently onwards, for he was elate with molten snow that the Poltiades had brought him from the Hills of Hap, and the Marn and Migris were swollen full with floods; and he bore us in his might past Kyph and Pir, and we saw the lights of Goolunza.

Soon we all slept except the helmsman, who kept the ship in the midstream of Yann.

When the sun rose the helmsman ceased to sing, for by song he cheered himself in the lonely night. When the song ceased we suddenly all awoke, and another took the helm, and the helmsman slept.

We knew that soon we should come to Mandaroon. We made a meal, and Mandaroon appeared. Then the captain commanded, and the sailors loosed again the greater sails, and the ship turned and left the stream of Yann and came into a harbour beneath the ruddy walls of Mandaroon. Then while the sailors went and gathered fruits I came alone to the gate of Mandaroon. A few huts were outside it, in which lived the guard. A sentinel with a long white beard was standing in the gate, armed with a rusty pike. He wore large spectacles, which were covered with dust. Through the gate I saw the city. A deathly stillness was over all of it. The ways seemed untrodden, and moss was thick on doorsteps; in the market-place huddled figures lay asleep. A scent of incense and burned poppies, and there was a hum of the echoes of distant bells. I said to the sentinel in the tongue of the region of Yann, "Why are they all asleep in this still city?"

He answered: "None may ask questions in this gate for fear they wake the people of the city. For when the people of this city wake the gods will die. And when the gods die men may dream no more." And

I began to ask him what gods that city worshipped, but he lifted his pike because none might ask questions there. So I left him and went back to the *Bird of the River*.

Certainly Mandaroon was beautiful with her white pinnacles peering over her ruddy walls and the green of her copper roofs.

When I came back again to the *Bird of the River,* I found the sailors were returned to the ship. Soon we weighed anchor, and sailed out again, and so came once more to the middle of the river. And now the sun was moving towards his heights, and there had reached us on the River Yann the song of those countless myriads of choirs that attend him in his progress round the world. For the little creatures that have many legs had spread their gauze wings easily on the air, as a man rests his elbows on a balcony and gave jubilant, ceremonial praises to the sun, or else they moved together on the air in wavering dances intricate and swift, or turned aside to avoid the onrush of some drop of water that a breeze had shaken from a jungle orchid, chilling the air and driving it before it, as it fell whirring in its rush to the earth; but all the while they sang triumphantly. "For the day is for us," they said, "whether our great and sacred father the Sun shall bring up more life like us from the marshes, or whether all the world shall end to-night." And there sang all those whose notes are known to human ears, as well as those whose far more numerous notes have never been heard by man.

To these a rainy day had been as an era of war that should desolate continents during all the lifetime of a man.

And there came out also from the dark and steaming jungle to behold and rejoice in the Sun the huge and lazy butterflies. And they danced, but danced idly, on the ways of the air, as some haughty queen of distant conquered lands might in her poverty and exile dance, in some encampment of the gipsies, for the mere bread to live by, but beyond that would never abate her pride to dance for a fragment more.

And the butterflies sung of strange and painted things, of purple orchids and of lost pink cities and the monstrous colours of the jungle's decay. And they, too, were among those whose voices are not discernible by human ears. And as they floated above the river, going from forest to forest, their splendour was matched by the inimical beauty of the birds who darted out to pursue them. Or sometimes they settled on the white and wax-like blooms of the plant that creeps and clambers about the trees of the forest; and their purple wings flashed out on the great blossoms as, when the caravans go from Nurl to Thace, the gleaming silks flash out upon the snow, where the crafty merchants spread them one by one to astonish the mountaineers of the Hills of Noor.

But upon men and beasts the sun sent a drowsiness. The river monsters along the river's marge lay dormant in the slime. The sailors pitched a pavilion, with golden tassels, for the captain upon the deck, and then went, all but the helmsman, under a sail that they had hung as an awning between two masts. Then they told tales to one another, each of his own city or of the miracles of his god, until all were fallen asleep. The captain offered me the shade of his pavilion with the gold tassels, and there we talked for a while, he telling me that he was taking merchandise to Perdondaris, and that he would take back to fair Belzoond things appertaining to the affairs of the sea. Then, as I watched through the pavilion's opening the brilliant birds and butterflies that crossed and recrossed over the river, I fell asleep, and dreamed that I was a monarch entering his capital underneath arches of flags, and all the musicians of the world were there, playing melodiously their instruments; but no one cheered.

In the afternoon, as the day grew cooler again, I awoke and found the captain buckling on his scimitar, which he had taken off him while he rested.

And now we were approaching the wide court of Astahahn, which opens upon the river. Strange boats of antique design were chained there to the steps. As we neared it we saw the open marble court, on three sides of which stood the city fronting on colonnades. And in the court and along the colonnades the people of that city walked with solemnity and care according to the rites of ancient ceremony. All in that city was of ancient device; the carving on the houses, which, when age had broken it remained unrepaired, was of the remotest times, and everywhere were represented in stone beasts that have long since passed away from Earth—the dragon, the griffin, and the hippogriffin, and the different species of gargoyle. Nothing was to be found, whether material or custom, that was new in Astahahn. Now they took no notice at all of us as we went by, but continued their processions and ceremonies in the ancient city, and the sailors, knowing their custom, took no notice of them. But I called, as we came near, to one who stood beside the water's edge, asking him what men did in Astahahn and what their merchandise was, and with whom they traded. He said, "Here we have fettered and manacled Time, who would otherwise slay the gods."

I asked him what gods they worshipped in that city, and he said, "All those gods whom Time has not yet slain." Then he turned from me and would say no more, but busied himself in behaving in accordance with ancient custom. And so, according to the will of Yann, we drifted onwards and left Astahahn, and we found in greater quantities such birds as prey on fishes. And they were very wonderful in their plumage, and they came not out of the jungle, but flew, with their long necks stretched out before them, and their legs lying on the wind behind straight up the river over the mid-stream.

And now the evening began to gather in. A thick white mist had appeared over the river, and was softly rising higher. It clutched at the trees with long impalpable arms, it rose higher and higher, chilling the air; and white shapes moved away into the jungle as though the ghosts of shipwrecked mariners were searching stealthily in the darkness for the spirits of evil that long ago had wrecked them on the Yann.

As the sun sank behind the field of orchids that grew on the matted summit of the jungle, the river monsters came wallowing out of the slime in which they had reclined during the heat of the day, and the great beasts of the jungle came down to drink. The butterflies a while since were gone to rest. In little narrow tributaries that we passed night seemed already to have fallen, though the sun which had disappeared from us had not yet set.

And now the birds of the jungle came flying home far over us, with the sunlight glistening pink upon their breasts, and lowered their pinions as soon as they saw the Yann, and dropped into the trees. And the widgeon began to go up the river in great companies, all whistling, and then would suddenly wheel and all go down again. And there shot by us the small and arrow-like teal; and we heard the manifold cries of flocks of geese, which the sailors told me had recently come in from crossing over the Lispasian ranges; every year they come by the same way, close by the peak of Mluna, leaving it to the left, and the mountain eagles know the way they come and—men say—the very hour, and every year they expect them by the same way as soon as the snows have fallen upon the Northern Plains. But soon it grew so dark that we saw these birds no more, and only heard the whirring of their wings, and of countless others besides, until they all settled down along the banks of the river, and it was the hour when the birds of the night went forth. Then the sailors lit the lanterns for the night, and huge moths appeared, flapping about the ship, and at moments their gorgeous colours would be revealed by the lanterns, then they would pass into the night again, where all was black. And again the sailors prayed, and thereafter we supped and slept, and the helmsman took our lives into his care.

When I awoke I found that we had indeed come to Perdondaris, that famous city. For there it stood upon the left of us, a city fair and notable, and all the more pleasant for our eyes to see after the jungle that was so long with us. And we were anchored by the marketplace, and the captain's merchandise was all displayed, and a merchant of Perdondaris stood looking at it. And the captain had his scimitar in his hand, and was beating with it in anger upon the deck, and the splinters were flying up from the white planks; for the merchant had offered him a price for his merchandise that the captain declared to be an insult to himself and his country's gods, whom he now said to be great and terrible gods, whose curses were to be dreaded. But the merchant waved his hands, which were of great fatness, showing his pink palms, and swore that of

himself he thought not at all, but only of the poor folk
in the huts beyond the city to whom he wished to sell
the merchandise for as low a price as possible, leaving no remuneration for himself. For the merchandise
was mostly the thick toomarund carpets that in the
winter keep the wind from the floor, and tollub which
the people smoke in pipes. Therefore the merchant
said if he offered a piffek more the poor folk must go
without their toomarunds when the winter came, and
without their tollub in the evenings, or else he and his
aged father must starve together. Thereat the captain
lifted his scimitar to his own throat, saying that he was
now a ruined man, and that nothing remained to him
but death. And while he was carefully lifting he beard
with his left hand, the merchant eyed the merchandise
again, and said that rather than see so worthy a captain die, a man for whom he had conceived an especial
love when first he saw the manner in which he handled
his ship, he and his aged father should starve together
and therefore he offered fifteen piffeks more.

When he said this the captain prostrated himself and
prayed to his gods that they might yet sweeten this
merchant's bitter heart—to his little lesser gods, to the
gods that bless Belzoond.

At last the merchant offered yet five piffeks more. Then
the captain wept, for he said that he was deserted of
his gods; and the merchant also wept, for he said that
he was thinking of his aged father, and of how soon he
would starve, and he hid his weeping face with both
his hands, and eyed the tollub again between his fingers. And so the bargain was concluded, and the merchant took the toomarund and tollub, paying for them
out of a great clinking purse. And these were packed
up into bales again, and three of the merchant's slaves
carried them upon their heads into the city. And all the

while the sailors had sat silent, cross-legged in a crescent upon the deck, eagerly watching the bargain, and now a murmur of satisfaction arose among them, and they began to compare it among themselves with other bargains that they had known. And I found out from them that there are seven merchants in Perdondaris, and that they had all come to the captain one by one before the bargaining began, and each had warned him privately against the others. And to all the merchants the captain had offered the wine of his own country, that they make in fair Belzoond, but could in no wise persuade them to it. But now that the bargain was over, and the sailors were seated at the first meal of the day, the captain appeared among them with a cask of that wine, and we broached it with care and all made merry together. And the captain was glad in his heart because he knew that he had much honour in the eyes of his men because of the bargain that he had made. So the sailors drank the wine of their native land, and soon their thoughts were back in fair Belzoond and the little neighbouring cities of Durl and Duz.

But for me the captain poured into a little glass some heavy yellow wine from a small jar which he kept apart among his sacred things. Thick and sweet it was, even like honey, yet there was in its heart a mighty, ardent fire which had authority over souls of men. It was made, the captain told me, with great subtlety by the secret craft of a family of six who lived in a hut on the mountains of Hian Min. Once in these mountains, he said, he followed the spoor of a bear, and he came suddenly on a man of that family who had hunted the same bear, and he was at the end of a narrow way with precipice all about him, and his spear was sticking in the bear, and the wound not fatal, and he had no other weapon. And the bear was walking towards the man, very slowly because his wound irked him—yet he was now very close. And what the captain did he would not say, but every year as soon as the snows are hard, and travelling is easy on the Hian Min, that man comes down to the market in the plains, and always leaves for the captain in the gate of fair Belzoond a vessel of that priceless secret wine.

And as I sipped the wine and the captain talked, I remembered me of stalwart noble things that I had long since resolutely planned, and my soul seemed to grow mightier within me and to dominate the whole tide of the Yann. It may be that I then slept. Or, if I did not, I do not now minutely recollect every detail of that morning's occupations. Towards evening, I awoke and wishing to see Perdondaris before we left in the morning, and being unable to wake the captain, I went ashore alone. Certainly Perdondaris was a powerful city; it was encompassed by a wall of great strength and altitude, having in it hollow ways for troops to walk in, and battlements along it all the way, and fifteen strong towers on it in every mile, and copper plaques low down where men could read them, telling in all the languages of those parts of the Earth—one language on each plaque—the tale of how an army once attacked Perdondaris and what befell that army. Then I entered Perdondaris and found all the people dancing, clad in brilliant silks, and playing on the tambang as they danced. For a fearful thunderstorm had terrified them while I slept, and the fires of death, they said, had danced over Perdondaris, and now the thunder had gone leaping away large and black and hideous, they said, over the distant hills, and had turned round snarling at them, showing his gleaming teeth, and had stamped, as he went, upon the hilltops until they rang as though they had been bronze. And often and again they stopped in their merry dances and prayed to the God they knew not, saying, "O, God that we know not, we thank Thee for sending the thunder back to his hills." And I went on and came to the market-place, and lying there upon the marble pavement I saw the merchant fast asleep and breathing heavily, with his face and the palms of his hands towards the sky, and slaves were fanning him to keep away the flies. And from the market-place I came to a silver temple and then to a palace of onyx, and there were many wonders in Perdondaris, and I would have stayed and seen them all, but as I came to the outer wall of the city I suddenly saw in it a huge ivory gate. For a while I paused and admired it, then I came nearer and perceived the dreadful truth. The gate was carved out of one solid piece!

I fled at once through the gateway and down to the ship, and even as I ran I thought that I heard far off on the hills behind me the tramp of the fearful beast by whom that mass of ivory was shed, who was perhaps even then looking for his other tusk. When I was on the ship again I felt safer, and I said nothing to the sailors of what I had seen.

And now the captain was gradually awakening. Now night was rolling up from the East and North, and only the pinnacles of the towers of Perdondaris still took the fallen sunlight. Then I went to the captain and told him quietly of the thing I had seen. And he questioned me at once about the gate, in a low voice, that the sailors might not know; and I told him how the weight of the thing was such that it could not have been brought from afar, and the captain knew that it had not been there a year ago. We agreed that such a beast could never have been killed by any assault of man, and that the gate must have been a fallen tusk, and one fallen near and recently. Therefore he decided that it were better to flee at once; so he commanded, and the sailors went to the sails, and others raised the anchor to the deck, and just as the highest pinnacle of marble lost the last rays of the sun we left Perdondaris, that famous city. And night came down and cloaked Perdondaris and hid it from our eyes, which as things have happened will never see it again; for I have heard since that something swift and wonderful has suddenly wrecked Perdondaris in a day—towers, and walls, and people.

And the night deepened over the River Yann, a night all white with stars. And with the night there arose the helmsman's song. As soon as he had prayed he began to sing to cheer himself all through the lonely night. But first he prayed, praying the helmsman's prayer. And this is what I remember of it, rendered into English with a very feeble equivalent of the rhythm that seemed so resonant in those tropic nights

To whatever god may hear.

Wherever there be sailors whether of river or sea: whether their way be dark or whether through storm: whether their perils be of beast or of rock: or from enemy lurking on land or pursuing on sea: wherever the tiller is cold or the helmsman stiff: wherever sailors sleep or helmsman watch: guard, guide, and return us to the old land, that has known us: to the far homes that we know.

To all the gods that are.

To whatever god may hear.

So he prayed, and there was silence. And the sailors laid them down to rest for the night. The silence deepened, and was only broken by the ripples of Yann that lightly touched our prow. Sometimes some monster of the river coughed.

Silence and ripples, ripples and silence again.

And then his loneliness came upon the helmsman, and he began to sing. And he sang the market songs of Durl and Duz, and the old dragon-legends of Belzoond.

Many a song he sang, telling to spacious and exotic Yann the little tales and trifles of his city of Durl. And the songs welled up over the black jungle and came into the clear cold air above, and the great bands of stars that looked on Yann began to know the affairs of Durl and Duz, and of the shepherds that dwelt in the fields between, and the flocks that they had, and the loves that they had loved, and all the little things that they hoped to do. And as I lay wrapped up in skins and blankets listening to those songs, and watching the fantastic shapes of the great trees like to black giants stalking through the night, I suddenly fell asleep.

When I awoke great mists were trailing away from the Yann. And the flow of the river was tumbling now tumultuously, and little waves appeared; for Yann had scented from afar the ancient crags of Glorm, and knew that their ravines lay cool before him wherein he should meet the merry wild Irillion rejoicing from fields of snow. So he shook off from him the torpid sleep that had come upon him in the hot and scented jungle, and forgot its orchids and its butterflies, and swept on turbulent, expectant, strong; and soon the snowy peaks of the Hills of Glorm came glittering into view. And now the sailors were waking up from sleep. Soon we all ate, and then the helmsman laid him down to sleep while a comrade took his place, and they all spread over him their choicest furs.

And in a while we heard the sound that the Irillion made as she came down dancing from the fields of snow.

And then we saw the ravine in the Hills of Glorm lying precipitous and smooth before us, into which we
were carried by the leaps of Yann. And now we left the
steamy jungle and breathed the mountain air; the sailors stood up and took deep breaths of it, and thought
of their own far-off Acroctian hills on which were
Durl and Duz—below them in the plains stands fair
Belzoond.

A great shadow brooded between the cliffs of Glorm, but the crags were shining above us like gnarled
moons, and almost lit the gloom. Louder and louder
came the Irillion's song, and the sound of her dancing
down from the fields of snow. And soon we saw her
white and full of mists, and wreathed with rainbows
delicate and small that she had plucked up near the
mountain's summit from some celestial garden of the
Sun. Then she went away seawards with the huge grey
Yann and the ravine widened, and opened upon the
world, and our rocking ship came through to the light
of day.

And all that morning and all the afternoon we passed
through the marshes of Pondoovery; and Yann widened there, and flowed solemnly and slowly, and the
captain bade the sailors beat on bells to overcome the
dreariness of the marshes.

At last the Irusian Mountains came in sight, nursing
the villages of Pen-Kai and Blut, and the wandering
streets of Mlo, where priests propitiate the avalanche
with wine and maize. Then the night came down over
the plains of Tlun, and we saw the lights of Cappa-
darnia. We heard the Pathnites beating upon drums
as we passed Imaut and Golzunda, then all but the
helmsman slept. And villages scattered along the
banks of the Yann heard all that night in the helms-

man's unknown tongue the little songs of cities that they know not.

I awoke before dawn with a feeling that I was unhappy before I remembered why. Then I recalled that by the evening of the approaching day, according to all forseen probabilities, we should come to Bar-Wul-Yann, and I should part from the captain and his sailors. And I had liked the man because he had given me of his yellow wine that was set apart among his sacred things, and many a story he had told me about his fair Belzoond between the Acrotian hills and the Hian Min. And I had liked the ways that his sailors had, and the prayers that they prayed at evening side by side, grudging not one another their alien gods. And I had a liking too for the tender way in which they often spoke of Durl and Duz, for it is good that men should love their native cities and the little hills that hold those cities up.

And I had come to know who would meet them when they returned to their homes, and where they thought the meetings would take place, some in a valley of the Acrotian hills where the road comes up from Yann, others in the gateway of one or another of the three cities, and others by the fireside in the home. And I thought of the danger that had menaced us all alike outside Perdondaris, a danger that, as things have happened, was very real.

And I thought too of the helmsman's cheery song in the cold and lonely night, and how he had held our lives in his careful hands. And as I thought of this the helmsman ceased to sing, and I looked up and saw a pale light had appeared in the sky, and the lonely night had passed; and the dawn widened, and the sailors awoke.

And soon we saw the tide of the Sea himself advancing resolute between Yann's borders, and Yann sprang lithely at him and they struggled a while; then Yann and all that was his were pushed back northwards, so that the sailors had to hoist the sails, and the wind being favourable, we still held onwards.

And we passed Gondara and Narl and Hoz. And we saw memorable, holy Golnuz, and heard the pilgrims praying.

When we awoke after the midday rest we were coming near to Nen, the last of the cities in the River Yann. And the jungle was all about us once again, and about Nen; but the great Mloon ranges stood up over all things, and watched the city from beyond the jungle.

Here we anchored, and the captain and I went up into the city and found that the Wanderers had come into Nen.

And the Wanderers were a weird, dark, tribe, that once in every seven years came down from the peaks of Mloon, having crossed by a pass that is known to them from some fantastic land that lies beyond. And the people of Nen were all outside their houses, and all stood wondering at their own streets. For the men and women of the Wanderers had crowded all the ways, and every one was doing some strange thing. Some danced astounding dances that they had learned from the desert wind, rapidly curving and swirling till the eye could follow no longer. Others played upon instruments beautiful wailing tunes that were full of horror, which souls had taught them lost by night in the desert, that strange far desert from which the Wanderers came.

None of their instruments were such as were known in Nen nor in any part of the region of the Yann; even the horns out of which some were made were of beasts that none had seen along the river, for they were barbed at the tips. And they sang, in the language of none, songs that seemed to be akin to the mysteries of night and to the unreasoned fear that haunts dark places.

Bitterly all the dogs of Nen distrusted them. And the Wanderers told one another fearful tales, for though no one in Nen knew aught of their language, yet they could see the fear on the listeners' faces, and as the tale wound on, the whites of their eyes showed vividly in terror as the eyes of some little beast whom the hawk has seized. Then the teller of the tale would smile and stop, and another would tell his story, and the teller of the first tale's lips would chatter with fear. And if some deadly snake chanced to appear the Wanderers would greet him like a brother, and the snake would seem to give his greetings to them before he passed on again. Once that most fierce and lethal of tropic snakes, the giant lythra, came out of the jungle and all down the street, the central street of Nen, and none of the Wanderers moved away from him, but they all played sonorously on drums, as though he had been a person of much honour; and the snake moved through the midst of them and smote none.

Even the Wanderers' children could do strange things, for if any one of them met with a child of Nen the two would stare at each other in silence with large grave eyes; then the Wanderers' child would slowly draw from his turban a live fish or snake. And the children of Nen could do nothing of that kind at all.

Much I should have wished to stay and hear the hymn with which they greet the night, that is answered by the wolves on the heights of Mloon, but it was now time to raise the anchor again that the captain might return from Bar-Wul-Yann upon the landward tide. So we went on board and continued down the Yann. And the captain and I spoke little, for we were thinking of our parting, which should be for long, and we watched instead the splendour of the westerning sun. For the sun was a ruddy gold, but a faint mist cloaked the jungle, lying low, and into it poured the smoke of the little jungle cities, and the smoke of them met together in the mist and joined into one haze, which became purple, and was lit by the sun, as the thoughts of men become hallowed by some great and sacred thing. Sometimes one column from a lonely house would rise up higher than the cities' smoke, and gleam by itself in the sun.

And now as the sun's last rays were nearly level, we saw the sight that I had come to see, for from two mountains that stood on either shore two cliffs of pink marble came out into the river, all glowing in the light of the low sun, and they were quite smooth and of mountainous altitude, and they nearly met, and Yann went tumbling between them and found the sea.

And this was Bar-Wul-Yann, the Gate of Yann, and in the distance through that barrier's gap I saw the azure indescribable sea, where little fishing-boats went gleaming by.

And the sunset and the brief twilight came, and the exultation of the glory of Bar-Wul-Yann was gone, yet still the pink cliffs glowed, the fairest marvel that the eye beheld-and this in a land of wonders. And soon the twilight gave place to the coming out of stars, and the colours of Bar-Wul-Yann went dwindling away. And the sight of those cliffs was to me as some chord of music that a master's hand had launched from the violin, and which carries to Heaven of Faery the tremulous spirits of men.

And now by the shore they anchored and went no farther, for they were sailors of the river and not of the sea, and knew the Yann but not the tides beyond.

And the time was come when the captain and I must part, he to go back again to his fair Belzoond in sight of the distant peaks of the Hian Min, and I to find my way by strange means back to those hazy fields that all poets know, wherein stand small mysterious cottages through whose windows, looking westwards, you may see the fields of men, and looking eastwards see glittering elfin mountains, tipped with snow, going range on range into the region of Myth, and beyond it into the kingdom of Fantasy, which pertain to the Lands of Dream. Long we should meet no more, for my fancy is weakening as the years slip by, and I go ever more seldom into the Lands of Dream. Then we clasped hands, uncouthly on his part, for it is not the method of greeting in his country, and he commended my soul to the care of his own gods, to his little lesser gods, the humble ones, to the gods that bless Belzoond.

Second Tale: A Shop In Go-By Street

I said I must go back to Yann again and see if *Bird of the River* still plies up and down and whether her bearded captain commands her still or whether he sits in the gate of fair Belzoond drinking at evening the marvellous yellow wine that the mountaineer brings down from the Hian Min. And I wanted to see the sailors again who came from Durl and Duz and to hear from their lips what befell Perdondaris when its doom came up without warning from the hills and fell on that famous city. And I wanted to hear the sailors pray at night each to his own god, and to feel the wind of the evening coolly arise when the sun went flaming away from that exotic river. For I thought never again to see the tide of Yann, but when I gave up politics not long ago the wings of my fancy strengthened, though they had erstwhile drooped, and I had hopes of coming behind the East once more where Yann like a proud white war-horse goes through the Lands of Dream.

Yet I had forgotten the way to those little cottages on the edge of the fields we know whose upper windows, though dim with antique cobwebs, look out on the fields we know not and are the starting-point of all adventure in all the Lands of Dream.

I therefore made enquiries. And so I came to be directed to the shop of a dreamer who lives not far from the Embankment in the City. Among so many streets as there are in the city it is little wonder that there is one that has never been seen before; it is named Goby Street and runs out of the Strand if you look very closely. Now when you enter this man's shop you do not go straight to the point but you ask him to sell you something, and if it is anything with which he can supply you he hands it you and wishes you good-morning. It is his way. And many have been deceived by asking for some unlikely thing, such as the oyster-shell from which was taken one of those single pearls that made the gates of Heaven in Revelations, and finding that the old man had it in stock.

He was comatose when I went into the shop, his heavy lids almost covered his little eyes; he sat, and his mouth was open. I said, "I want some of Abama and Pharpah, rivers of Damascus." "How much?" he said. "Two and a half yards of each, to be delivered to my flat." "That is very tiresome," he muttered, "very tiresome. We do not stock it in that quantity." "Then I will take all you have," I said.

He rose laboriously and looked among some bottles. I saw one labelled: Nilos, river of AEgyptos; and others Holy Ganges, Phlegethon, Jordan; I was almost afraid he had it, when I heard him mutter again, "This is very tiresome," and presently he said, "We are out of it." "Then," I said, "I wish you to tell me the way to those little cottages in whose upper chambers poets look out upon the fields we know not, for I wish to go into the Land of Dream and to sail once more upon mighty, sea-like Yann."

At that he moved heavily and slowly in way-worn carpet slippers, panting as he went, to the back part of his shop, and I went with him. This was a dingy lumber-room full of idols: the near end was dingy and dark but at the far end was a blue caerulean glow in which stars seemed to be shining and the heads of the idols glowed. "This," said the fat old man in carpet slippers, "is the heaven of the gods who sleep." I asked him what gods slept and he mentioned names that I had never heard as well as names that I knew. "All those," he said, "that are not worshipped now are asleep."

"Then does Time not kill the gods?" I said to him and he answered, "No. But for three or four thousand years a god is worshipped and for three or four he sleeps. Only Time is wakeful always."

"But they that teach us of new gods"—I said to him, "are they not new?"

"They hear the old ones stirring in their sleep being about to wake, because the dawn is breaking and the priests crow. These are the happy prophets: unhappy are they that hear some old god speak while he sleeps still being deep in slumber, and prophesy and prophesy and no dawn comes, they are those that men stone saying, 'Prophesy where this stone shall hit you, and this.'"

"Then shall Time never slay the gods," I said. And he answered, "They shall die by the bedside of the last man. Then Time shall go mad in his solitude and shall not know his hours from his centuries of years and they shall clamour round him crying for recognition and he shall lay his stricken hands on their heads and stare at them blindly and say, 'My children, I do not know you one from another,' and at these words of Time empty worlds shall reel."

And for some while then I was silent, for my imagination went out into those far years and looked back at me and mocked me because I was the creature of a day.

Suddenly I was aware by the old man's heavy breathing that he had gone to sleep. It was not an ordinary shop: I feared lest one of his gods should wake and call for him: I feared many things, it was so dark, and one or two of those idols were something more than grotesque. I shook the old man hard by one of his arms.

"Tell me the way to the cottages," I said, "on the edge of the fields we know."

"I don't think we can do that," he said.

"Then supply me," I said, "with the goods."

That brought him to his senses. He said, "You go out by the back door and turn to the right"; and he opened a little, old, dark door in the wall through which I went, and he wheezed and shut the door. The back of the shop was of incredible age. I saw in antique characters upon a mouldering board, "Licensed to sell weasels and jade earrings." The sun was setting now and shone on little golden spires that gleamed along the roof which had long ago been thatched and with a wonderful straw. I saw that the whole of Go-by Street had the same strange appearance when looked at from behind. The pavement was the same as the pavement of which I was weary and of which so many thousand miles lay the other side of those houses, but the street was of most pure untrampled grass with such marvellous flowers in it that they lured downward from great heights the flocks of butterflies as they traveled by, going I know not whence. The other side of the street there was pavement again but no houses of any kind, and what there was in place of them I did not stop to see, for I turned to my right and walked along the back of Go-by Street till I came to the open fields and the gardens of the cottages that I sought. Huge flowers went up out of these gardens like slow rockets and burst into purple blooms and stood there huge and radiant on six-foot stalks and softly sang strange songs. Others came up beside them and bloomed and began singing too. A very old witch came out of her cottage by the back door and into the garden in which I stood.

"What are these wonderful flowers?" I said to her.

"Hush! Hush!" she said, "I am putting the poets to bed. These flowers are their dreams."

And in a lower voice I said: "What wonderful songs are they singing?" and she said, "Be still and listen."

And I listened and found they were singing of my own childhood and of things that happened there so far away that I had quite forgotten them till I heard the wonderful song.

"Why is the song so faint?" I said to her.

"Dead voices," she said, "Dead voices," and turned back again to her cottage saying: "Dead voices" still, but softly for fear that she should wake the poets. "They sleep so badly while they live," she said.

I stole on tiptoe upstairs to the little room from whose windows, looking one way, we see the fields we know and, looking another, those hilly lands that I sought—almost I feared not to find them. I looked at once toward the mountains of faery; the afterglow of the sunset flamed on them, their avalanches flashed on their violet slopes coming down tremendous from emerald peaks of ice; and there was the old gap in the blue-grey hills above the precipice of amethyst whence one sees the Lands of Dream.

All was still in the room where the poets slept when I came quietly down. The old witch sat by a table with a lamp, knitting a splendid cloak of gold and green for a king that had been dead a thousand years.

"Is it any use," I said, "to the king that is dead that you sit and knit him a cloak of gold and green?"

"Who knows?" she said.

"What a silly question to ask," said her old black cat who lay curled by the fluttering fire.

Already the stars were shining on that romantic land when I closed the witch's door; already the glow-worms were mounting guard for the night around those magical cottages. I turned and trudged for the gap in the blue-grey mountains.

Already when I arrived some colour began to show in the amethyst precipice below the gap although it was not yet morning. I heard a rattling and sometimes caught a flash from those golden dragons far away below me that are the triumph of the goldsmiths of Sirdoo and were given life by the ritual incantations of the conjurer Amargrarn. On the edge of the opposite cliff, too near I thought for safety, I saw the ivory palace of Singanee that mighty elephant-hunter; small lights appeared in windows, the slaves were awake, and beginning with heavy eyelids the work of the day.

And now a ray of sunlight topped the world. Others than I must describe how it swept from the amethyst cliff the shadow of the black one that opposed it, how that one shaft of sunlight pierced the amethyst for leagues, and how the rejoicing colour leaped up to welcome the light and shot back a purple glow on the walls of the palace of ivory while down in that incredible ravine the golden dragons still played in the darkness.

At this moment a female slave came out by a door of the palace and tossed a basket-full of sapphires over the edge. And when day was manifest on those marvellous heights and the flare of the amethyst precipice filled the abyss, then the elephant-hunter arose in his ivory palace and took his terrific spear and going out by a landward door went forth to avenge Perdondaris

I turned then and looked upon the lands of Dream, and the thin white mist that never rolls quite away was shifting in the morning. Rising like isles above it I saw the Hills of Hap and the city of copper, old, deserted Bethmoora, and Utnar Vehi and Kyph and Mandaroon and the wandering leagues of Yann. Rather I guessed than saw the Hian Min whose imperturbable and aged heads scarce recognize for more than clustered mounds the round Acroctian hills, that are heaped about their feet and that shelter, as I remembered, Durl and Duz. But most clearly I discerned that ancient wood through which one going down to the bank of Yann whenever the moon is old may come on *Bird of the River* anchored there, waiting three days for travellers, as has been prophesied of her. And as it was now that season I hurried down from the gap in the blue-grey hills by an elfin path that was coeval with fable, and came by means of it to the edge of the wood. Black though the darkness was in that ancient wood the beasts that moved in it were blacker still. It is very seldom that any dreamer travelling in Lands of Dream is ever seized by these beasts, and yet I ran; for if a man's spirit is seized in the Lands of Dream his body may survive it for many years and well know the beasts that mouthed him far away and the look in their little eyes and the smell of their breath; that is why the recreation field at Hanwell is so dreadfully trodden into restless paths.

And so I came at last to the sea-like flood of proud, tremendous Yann, with whom there tumbled streams from incredible lands—with these he went by singing. Singing he carried drift-wood and whole trees, fallen in far-away, unvisited forests, and swept them mightily by, but no sign was there either out in the river or in the olden anchorage near by of the ship I came to see.

And I built myself a hut and roofed it over with the huge abundant leaves of a marvellous weed and ate the meat that grows on the targar-tree and waited there three days. And all day long the river tumbled by and all night long the tolulu-bird sang on and the huge fireflies had no other care than to pour past in torrents of dancing sparks, and nothing rippled the surface of the Yann by day and nothing disturbed the tolulu-bird by night. I know not what I feared for the ship I sought and its friendly captain who came from fair Belzoond and its cheery sailors out of Durl and Duz; all day long I looked for it on the river and listened for it by night until the dancing fireflies danced me to sleep. Three times only in those three nights the tolulu-bird was scared and stopped his song, and each time I awoke with a start and found no ship and saw that he was only scared by the dawn. Those indescribable dawns upon the Yann came up like flames in some land over the hills where a magician burns by secret means enormous amethysts in a copper pot. I used to watch them in wonder while no bird sang—till all of a sudden the sun came over a hill and every bird but one began to sing, and the tolulu-bird slept fast, till out of an opening eye he saw the stars.

I would have waited three more days, but on the third day I had gone in my loneliness to see the very spot where first I met *Bird of the River* at her anchorage with her bearded captain sitting on the deck. And as I looked at the black mud of the harbour and pictured in my mind that band of sailors whom I had not seen for two years, I saw an old hulk peeping from the mud. The lapse of centuries seemed partly to have rotted and partly to have buried in the mud all but the prow of the boat and on the prow I faintly saw a name. I read it slowly—it was *Bird of the River*. And then I knew that, while in Ireland and London two years had barely passed over my head, ages had gone over the region of Yann and wrecked and rotted that once familiar ship, and buried years ago the bones of the youngest of my friends, who so often sang to me of Durl and Duz or told the dragon-legends of Belzoond. For beyond the world we know there roars a hurricane of centuries whose echo only troubles—though sorely—our fields; while elsewhere there is calm. I stayed a moment by that battered hulk and said a prayer for whatever may be immortal of those who were wont to sail it down the Yann, and I prayed for them to the gods to whom they loved to pray, to the little lesser gods that bless Belzoond. Then leaving the hut that I built to those ravenous years I turned my back to the Yann and entering the forest at evening just as its orchids were opening their petals to perfume the night came out of it in the morning, and passed that day along the amethyst gulf by the gap in the blue-grey mountains. I wondered if Singanee, that mighty elephant-hunter, had returned again with his spear to his lofty ivory palace or if his doom had been one with that of Perdondaris. I saw a merchant at a small back door selling new sapphires as I passed the palace, then I went on and came as twilight fell to those small cottages where the elfin mountains are in sight of the fields we know. And I went to the old witch that I had seen before and she sat in her parlour with a red shawl round her shoulders still knitting the golden cloak, and faintly through one of her windows the elfin mountains shone and I saw again through another the fields we know.

"Tell me something," I said, "of this strange land!"

"How much do you know?" she said. "Do you know that dreams are illusion?"

"Of course I do," I said. "Every one knows that."

"Oh no they don't," she said, "the mad don't know it."

"That is true," I said.

"And do you know," she said, "that Life is illusion?"

"Of course it is not," I said. "Life is real, Life is earnest—."

At that the witch and her cat (who had not moved from her old place by the hearth) burst into laughter. I stayed some time, for there was much that I wished to ask, but when I saw that the laughter would not stop I turned and went away.

Third Tale: The Avenger of Perdondaris

I was rowing on the Thames not many days after my return from the Yann and drifting eastwards with the fall of the tide away from Westminster Bridge, near which I had hired my boat. All kinds of things were on the water with me—sticks drifting, and huge boats— and I was watching, so absorbed the traffic of that great river that I did not notice I had come to the City until I looked up and saw that part of the Embankment that is nearest to Go-by Street. And then I suddenly wondered what befell Singanee, for there was a stillness about his ivory palace when I passed it by, which made me think that he had not then returned. And though I had seen him go forth with his terrific spear, and mighty elephant-hunter though he was, yet his was a fearful quest for I knew that it was none other than to avenge Perdondaris by slaying that monster with the single tusk who had overthrown it suddenly in a day. So I tied up my boat as soon as I came to some steps, and landed and left the Embankment, and about the third street I came to I began to look for the opening of Go-by Street; it is very narrow, you hardly notice it at first, but there it was, and soon I was in the old man's shop. But a young man leaned over the counter. He had no information to give me about the old man—he was sufficient in himself. As to the little old door in the back of the shop, "We know nothing about that, sir." So I had to talk to him and humour him. He had for sale on the counter an instrument for picking up a lump of sugar in a new way. He was pleased when I looked at it and he began to praise it. I asked him what was the use of it, and he said that it was of no use but that it had only been invented a week ago and was quite new and was made of real silver and was being very much bought. But all the while I was straying towards the back of the shop. When I enquired about the idols there he said that they were some of the season's novelties and were a choice selection of mascots; and while I made a pretence of selecting one I suddenly saw the wonderful old door. I was through it at once and the young shop-keeper after me. No one was more surprised than he when he saw the street of grass and the purple flowers on it; he ran across in his frock-coat on to the opposite pavement and only just stopped in time, for the world ended there. Looking downward over the pavement's edge he saw, instead of accustomed kitchen-windows, white clouds and a wide, blue sky. I led him to the old back door of the shop, looking pale and in need of air, and pushed him lightly and he went limply through, for I thought the air was better for him on the side of the street that he knew. As soon as the door was shut on that astonished man I turned to the right and went along the street till I saw the gardens and the cottages, and a little red patch moving in a garden, which I knew to be the old witch wearing her shawl.

"Come for a change of illusion again?" she said.

"I have come from London," I said. "And I want to see Singanee. I want to go to his ivory palace over the elfin mountains where the amethyst precipice is."

"Nothing like changing your illusions," she said, "or you grow tired. London's a fine place but one wants to see the elfin mountains sometimes."

"Then you know London?" I said.

"Of course I do," she said. "I can dream as well as you. You are not the only person that can imagine London." Men were toiling dreadfully in her garden; it was in the heat of the day and they were digging with spades; she suddenly turned from me to beat one of them over the back with a long black stick that she carried. "Even my poets go to London sometimes," she said to me.

"Why did you beat that man?" I said.

"To make him work," she answered.

"But he is tired," I said.

"Of course he is," said she.

And I looked and saw that the earth was difficult and dry and that every spadeful that the tired men lifted was full of pearls; but some men sat quite still and watched the butterflies that flitted about the garden and the old witch did not beat them with her stick. And when I asked her who the diggers were she said, "These are my poets, they are digging for pearls." And when I asked her what so many pearls were for she said to me: "To feed the pigs of course."

"But do the pigs like pearls?" I said to her.

"Of course they don't," she said. And I would have pressed the matter further but the old black cat had come out of the cottage and was looking at me whimsically and saying nothing so that I knew I was asking silly questions. And I asked instead why some of the poets were idle and were watching butterflies without being beaten. And she said: "The butterflies know where the pearls are hidden and they are waiting for one to alight above the buried treasure. They cannot dig until they know where to dig." And all of a sudden a faun came out of a rhododendron forest and began to dance upon a disk of bronze in which a fountain was set; and the sound of his two hooves dancing on the bronze was beautiful as bells.

"Tea-bell," said the witch; and all the poets threw down their spades and followed her into the house, and I followed them; but the witch and all of us followed the black cat, who arched his back and lifted his tail and walked along the garden-path of blue enamelled tiles and through the black-thatched porch and the open, oaken door and into a little room where tea was ready. And in the garden the flowers began to sing and the fountain tinkled on the disk of bronze. And I learned that the fountain came from an otherwise unknown sea, and sometimes it threw gilded fragments up from the wrecks of unheard-of galleons, foundered in storms of some sea that was nowhere in the world; or battered to bits in wars waged with we know not whom. Some said that it was salt because of the sea and others that it was salt with mariners' tears. And some of the poets took large flowers out of vases and threw their petals all about the room, and others talked two at a time and other sang. "Why they are only children after all," I said.

"Only children!" repeated the old witch who was pouring out cowslip wine.

"*Only* children," said the old black cat. And every one laughed at me.

"I sincerely apologize," I said. "I did not mean to say it. I did not intend to insult any one."

"Why he knows nothing at all," said the old black cat. And everybody laughed till the poets were put to bed.

And then I took one look at the fields we know, and turned to the other window that looks on the elfin mountains. And the evening looked like a sapphire. And I saw my way though the fields were growing dim, and when I found it I went downstairs and through the witch's parlour, and out of doors and came that night to the palace of Singanee.

Lights glittered through every crystal slab—and all were uncurtained—in the palace of ivory. The sounds were those of a triumphant dance. Very haunting indeed was the booming of a bassoon, and like the dangerous advance of some galloping beast were the blows wielded by a powerful man on the huge, sonourous drum. It seemed to me as I listened that the contest of Singanee with the more than elephantine destroyer of Perdondaris had already been set to music. And as I walked in the dark along the amethyst precipice I suddenly saw across it a curved white bridge. It was one ivory tusk. And I knew it for the triumph of Singanee. I knew at once that this curved mass of ivory that had been dragged by ropes to bridge the abyss was the twin of the ivory gate that once Perdondaris had, and had itself been the destruction of that once famous city—towers and walls and people. Already men had begun to hollow it and to carve human figures life-size along its sides. I walked across it; and half way across, at the bottom of the curve, I met a few of the carvers fast asleep. On the opposite cliff by the palace lay the thickest end of the tusk and I came down a ladder which leaned against the tusk for they had not yet carved steps.

Outside the ivory palace it was as I had supposed and the sentry at the gate slept heavily; and though I asked of him permission to enter the palace he only muttered a blessing on Singanee and fell asleep again. It was evident that he had been drinking bak. Inside the ivory hall I met with servitors who told me that any stranger was welcome there that night, because they extolled the triumph of Singanee. And they offered me bak to drink to commemorate the splendour but I did not know its power nor whether a little or much prevailed over a man so I said that I was under an oath to a god to drink nothing beautiful; and they asked me if he could not be appeased by a prayer, and I said, "In nowise," and went towards the dance; and they commiserated me and abused that god bitterly, thinking to please me thereby, and then they fell to drinking bak to the glory of Singanee. Outside the curtains that hung before the dance there stood a chamberlain and when I told him that though a stranger there, yet I was well known to Mung and Sish and Kib, the gods of Pegana, whose signs I made, he bade me ample welcome. Therefore I questioned him about my clothes asking if they were not unsuitable to so august an occasion and he swore by the spear that had slain the destroyer of Perdondaris that Singanee would think it a shameful thing that any stranger not unknown to the gods should enter the dancing hall unsuitably clad; and therefore he led me to another room and took silken robes out of an old sea-chest of black and seamy oak with green copper hasps that were set with a few pale sapphires, and requested me to choose a suitable robe. And I chose a bright green robe, with an under-robe of light blue which was seen here and there, and a light blue sword-belt. I also wore a cloak that was dark purple with two thin strips of dark-blue along the border and a row of large dark sapphires sewn along the purple between them; it hung down from my shoulders behind me. Nor would the chamberlain of Singanee let me take any less than this, for he said that not even a stranger, on that night, could be allowed to stand in the way of his master's munificence which he was pleased to exercise in honour of his victory. As soon as I was attired we went to the dancing hall and the first thing that I saw in that tall, scintillant chamber was the huge form of Singanee standing among the dancers and the heads of the men no higher than his waist. Bare were the huge arms that had held the spear that had avenged Perdondaris. The chamberlain led me to him and I bowed, and said that I gave thanks to the gods to whom he looked for protection; and he said that he had heard my gods well spoken of by those accustomed to pray but this he said only of courtesy, for he knew not whom they were.

Singanee was simply dressed and only wore on his head a plain gold band to keep his hair from falling over his forehead, the ends of the gold were tied in the back with a bow of purple silk. But all his queens wore crowns of great magnificence, though whether they were crowned as the queens of Singanee or whether queens were attracted there from the thrones of distant lands by the wonder of him and the splendour I did not know.

All there wore silken robes of brilliant colours and the feet of all were bare and very shapely for the custom of boots was unknown in those regions. And when they

saw that my big toes were deformed in the manner of
Europeans, turning inwards towards the others instead of being straight, one or two asked sympatheti-
cally if an accident had befallen me. And rather than
tell them truly that deforming out big toes was our
custom and our pleasure I told them that I was under
the curse of a malignant god at whose feet I had ne-
glected to offer berries in infancy. And to some extent
I justified myself, for Convention is a god though his
ways are evil; and had I told them the truth I would not
have been understood. They gave me a lady to dance
with who was of marvellous beauty, she gold me that
her name was Saranoora, a princess from the North,
who had been sent as tribute to the palace of Singanee.
And partly she danced as Europeans dance and partly
as the fairies of the waste who lure, as legend has it,
lost travellers to their doom. And if I could get thirty
heathen men out of fantastic lands, with their long
black hair and little elfin eyes and instruments of music even unknown to Nebuchadnezzar the King; and if
I could make them play those tunes that I heard in the
ivory palace on some lawn, gentle reader, at evening
near your house then you would understand the beauty of Saranoora and the blaze of light and colour in
that stupendous hall and the lithesome movement of
those mysterious queens that danced round Singanee.
Then gentle reader you would be gentle no more but
the thoughts that run like leopards over the far free
lands would come leaping into your head even were it
London, yes, even in London: you would rise up then
and beat your hands on the wall with its pretty pattern
of flowers, in the hope that the bricks might break and
reveal the way to that palace of ivory by the amethyst
gulf where the golden dragons are. For there have
been men who have burned prisons down that the
prisoners might escape, and even such incendiaries

those dark musicians are who dangerously burn down custom that the pining thoughts may go free. Let your elders have no fear, have no fear. I will not play those tunes in any streets we know. I will not bring those strange musicians here, I will only whisper the way to the Lands of Dream, and only a few frail feet shall find the way, and I shall dream alone of the beauty of Saranoora and sometimes sigh. We danced on and on at the will of the thirty musicians, but when the stars were paling and the wind that knew the dawn was ruffling up the edge of the skirts of night, then Saranoora the princess of the North led me out into a garden. Dark groves of trees were there which filled the night with perfume and guarded night's mysteries from the arising dawn. There floated over us, wandering in that garden, the triumphant melody of those dark musicians, whose origin was unguessed even by those that dwelt there and knew the Lands of Dream. For only a moment once sang the tolulu-bird, for the festival of that night had scared him and he was silent. For only a moment once we heard him singing in some far grove because the musicians rested and our bare feet made no sound; for a moment we heard that bird of which once our nightingale dreamed and handed on the tradition to his children. And Saranoora told me that they have named the bird the Sister of Song; but for the musicians, who presently played again, she said they had no name, for no one knew who they were or from what country. Then some one sang quite near us in the darkness to an instrument of strings telling of Singanee and his battle against the monster. And soon we saw him sitting on the ground and singing to the night of that spear-thrust that had found the thumping heart of the destroyer of Perdondaris; and we stopped awhile and asked him who had seen so memorable a struggle and he answered none but Singanee and he whose tusk had scattered Perdondaris, and now the last was dead. And when we asked him if Singanee had told him of the struggle he said that that proud hunter would say no word about it and that therefore his mighty deed was given to the poets and become their trust forever, and he struck again his instrument of strings and sang on.

When the strings of pearls that hung down from her neck began to gleam all over Saranoora I knew that dawn was near and that that memorable night was all but gone. And at last we left the garden and came to the abyss to see the sunrise shine on the amethyst cliff. And at first it lit up the beauty of Saranoora and then it topped the world and blazed upon those cliffs of amethyst until it dazzled our eyes, and we turned from it and saw the workman going out along the tusk to hollow it and to carve a balustrade of fair professional figures. And those who had drunken bak began to awake and to open their dazzled eyes at the amethyst precipice and to rub them and turn them away. And now those wonderful kingdoms of song that the dark musicians established all night by magical chords dropped back again to the sway of that ancient silence who ruled before the gods, and the musicians wrapped their cloaks about them and covered up their marvellous instruments and stole away to the plains; and no one dared ask them whither they went or why they dwelt there, or what god they served. And the dance stopped and all the queens departed. And then the female slave came out again by a door and emptied her basket of sapphires down the abyss as I saw her do before. Beautiful Saranoora said that those great queens would never wear their sapphires more than once and that every day at noon a merchant from the mountains sold new ones for that evening. Yet I suspected that something more than extravagance lay at

the back of that seemingly wasteful act of tossing sapphires into an abyss, for thee were in the depths of it
those two dragons of gold of whom nothing seemed
to be known. And I thought, and I think so still, that
Singanee, terrific though he was in war with the ele-
phants, from whose tusks he had built his palace, well
knew and even feared those dragons in the abyss, and
perhaps valued those priceless jewels less than he valued his queens, and that he to whom so many lands
paid beautiful tribute out of their dread of his spear,
himself paid tribute to the golden dragons. Whether
those dragons had wings I could not see; nor, if they
had, could I tell if they could bear that weight of solid gold from the abyss; nor by what paths they could
crawl from it did I know. And I know not what use to
a golden dragon should sapphires be or a queen. Only
it seemed strange to me that so much wealth of jewels should be thrown by command of a man who had
nothing to fear—to fall flashing and changing their
colours at dawn into an abyss.

I do not know how long we lingered there watching the sunrise on those miles of amethyst. And it is
strange that that great and famous wonder did not
move me more than it did, but my mind was dazzled
by the fame of it and my eyes were actually dazzled
by the blaze, and as often happens I thought more of
little things and remember watching the daylight in
the solitary sapphire that Saranoora had and that she
wore upon her finger in a ring. Then, the dawn wind
being all about her, she said that she was cold and
turned back into the ivory palace. And I feared that
we might never meet again, for time moves differently
over the Lands of Dream than over the fields we know;
like ocean-currents going different ways and bearing
drifting ships. And at the doorway of the ivory palace
I turned to say farewell and yet I found no words that

were suitable to say. And often now when I stand in other lands I stop and think of many things to have said; yet all I said was "Perhaps we shall meet again." And she said that it was likely that we should often meet for that this was a little thing for the gods to permit not knowing that the gods of the Lands of Dream have little power upon the fields we know. Then she went in through the doorway. And having exchanged for my own clothes again the raiment that the chamberlain had given me I turned from the hospitality of mighty Singanee and set my face towards the fields we know. I crossed that enormous tusk that had been the end of Perdondaris and met the artists carving it as I went; and some by way of greeting as I passed extolled Singanee, and in answer I gave honour to his name. Daylight had not yet penetrated wholly to the bottom of the abyss but the darkness was giving place to a purple haze and I could faintly see one golden dragon there. Then looking once towards the ivory palace, and seeing no one at the windows, I turned sorrowfully away, and going by the way that I knew passed through the gap in the mountains and down their slopes till I came again in sight of the witch's cottage. And as I went to the upper window to look for the fields we know, the witch spoke to me; but I was cross, as one newly waked from sleep, and I would not answer her. Then the cat questioned me as to whom I had met, and I answered him that in the fields we know cats kept their place and did not speak to man. And then I came downstairs and walked straight out of the door, heading for Go-by Street. "You are going the wrong way," the witch called through the window; and indeed I had sooner gone back to the ivory palace again, but I had no right to trespass any further on the hospitality of Singanee and one cannot stay always in the Lands of Dream, and what knowledge had that old witch of the call of the fields we know or the little though many snares that bind our feet therein? So I paid no heed to her, but kept on, and came to Go-by Street. I saw the house with the green door some way up the street but thinking that the near end of the street was closer to the Embankment where I had left my boat I tried the first door I came to, a cottage thatched like the rest, with little golden spires along the roof-ridge, and strange birds sitting there and preening marvellous feathers. The door opened, and to my surprise I found myself in what seemed like a shepherd's cottage; a man who was sitting on a log of wood in a little low dark room said something to me in an alien language. I muttered something and hurried through to the street. The house was thatched in front as well as behind. There were not golden spires in front, no marvellous birds; but there was no pavement. There was a row of houses, byres, and barns but no other sign of a town. Far off I saw one or two little villages. Yet there was the river—and no doubt the Thames, for it was the width of the Thames and had the curves of it, if you can imagine the Thames in that particular spot without a city around it, without any bridges, and the Embankment fallen in. I saw that there had happened to me permanently and in the light of day some such thing as happens to a man, but to a child more often, when he awakes before morning in some strange room and sees a high, grey window where the door ought to be and unfamiliar objects in wrong places and though knowing where he is yet knows not how it can be that the place should look like that.

A flock of sheep came by me presently looking the same as ever, but the man who led them had a wild, strange look. I spoke to him and he did not understand me. Then I went down to the river to see if my boat was there and at the very spot where I had left it, in the mud (for the tide was low) I saw a half-buried piece of blackened wood that might have been part of a boat, but I could not tell. I began to feel that I had missed the world. It would be a strange thing to travel from far away to see London and not be able to find it among all the roads that lead there, but I seemed to have travelled in Time and to have missed it among the centuries. And when as I wandered over the grassy hills I came on a wattled shrine that was thatched with straw and saw a lion in it more worn with time than even the Sphinx at Gizeh and when I knew it for one of the four in Trafalgar Square then I saw that I was stranded far away in the future with many centuries of treacherous years between me and anything that I had known. And then I sat on the grass by the worn paws of the lion to think out what to do. And I decided to go back through Go-by Street and, since there was nothing left to keep me any more to the fields we know, to offer myself as a servant in the palace of Singanee, and to see again the face of Saranoora and those famous, wonderful, amethystine dawns upon the abyss where the golden dragons play. And I stayed no longer to look for remains of the ruins of London; for there is little pleasure in seeing wonderful things if there is no one at all to hear of them and to wonder. So I returned at once to Go-by Street, the little row of huts, and saw no other record that London had been except that one stone lion. I went to the right house this time. It was very much altered and more like one of those huts that one sees on Salisbury plain than a shop in the city of London, but I found it by counting the houses in the street for it was still a row of houses though pavement and city were gone. And it was still a shop. A very different shop to the one I knew, but things were for sale there—shepherd's crooks, food, and rude axes. And a man with long hair was there who was clad in skins. I did not speak to him for I did not know his language. He said to me something that sounded like "Everkike." It conveyed no meaning to me; but when he looked towards one of his buns, light suddenly dawned in my mind, and I knew that England was even England still and that still she was not conquered, and that though they had tired of London they still held to their land; for the words that the man had said were, "Av er kike," and then I knew that that very language that was carried to distant lands by the old, triumphant cockney was spoken still in his birthplace and that neither his politics nor his enemies had destroyed him after all these thousand years. I had always disliked the Cockney dialect—and with the arrogance of the Irishman who hears from rich and poor the English of the splendour of Elizabeth; and yet when I heard those words my eyes felt sore as with impending tears—it should be remembered how far away I was. I think I was silent for a little while. Suddenly I saw that the man who kept the shop was asleep. That habit was strangely like the ways of a man who if he were then alive would be (if I could judge from the time-worn look of the lion) over a thousand years old. But then how old was I? It is perfectly clear that Time moves over the Lands of Dream swifter or slower than over the fields we know. For the dead, and the long dead, live again in our dreams; and a dreamer passes through the events of days in a single moment of the Town-Hall's clock. Yet logic did not aid me and my mind was puzzled. While the old man slept—and strangely like in face he was to the old man who had shown me first the little, old backdoor—I went to the far end of his wattled shop. There was a door of a sort on leather hinges. I pushed it open and there I was again under the notice-board at the back of the shop, at least the back of Go-by Street had not changed. Fantastic and remote though this grass street was with its purple flowers and the golden spires, and the world ending at its opposite pavement, yet I breathed more happily to see something again that I had seen before. I thought I had lost forever the world I knew, and now that I was at the back of Go-by Street again I felt the loss less than when I was standing where familiar things ought to be; and I turned my mind to what was left me in the vast Lands of Dream and thought of Sara-noora. And when I saw the cottages again I felt less lonely even at the thought of the cat though he gener-ally laughed at the things I said. And the first thing that I saw when I saw the witch was that I had lost the world and was going back for the rest of my days to the palace of Singanee. And the first thing that she said was: "Why! You've been through the wrong door," quite kindly for she saw how unhappy I looked. And I said, "Yes, but it's all the same street. The whole street's altered and London's gone and the people I used to know and the houses I used to rest in, and everything; and I'm tired."

"What did you want to go through the wrong door for?" she said.

"O, that made no difference," I said.

"O, didn't it?" she said in a contradictory way.

"Well I wanted to get to the near end of the street so as to find my boat quickly by the Embankment. And now my boat, and the Embankment and—and—."

"Some people are always in such a hurry," said the old black cat. And I felt too unhappy to be angry and I said nothing more.

And the old witch said, "Now which way do you want to go?" and she was talking rather like a nurse to a small child. And I said, "I have nowhere to go."

And she said, "Would you rather go home or go to the ivory palace of Singanee." And I said, "I've got a headache, and I don't want to go anywhere, and I'm tired of the Lands of Dream."

"Then suppose you try going in through the right door," she said.

"That's no good," I said. "Everyone's dead and gone, and they're selling buns there."

"What do you know about Time?" she said.

"Nothing," answered the old, black cat, though nobody spoke to him.

"Run along," said the old witch.

So I turned and trudged away to Go-by Street again. I was very tired. "What does he know about anything?" said the old black cat behind me. I knew what he was going to say next. He waited a moment and then said, "Nothing." When I looked over my shoulder he was strutting back to the cottage. And when I got to Go-by Street I listlessly opened the door through which I had just now come. I saw no use in doing it, I just did wearily as I was told. And the moment I got inside I saw it was just the same as of old, and the sleepy old man was there who sold idols. And I bought a vulgar thing that I did not want, for the sheer joy of seeing accustomed things. And when I turned from Go-by Street which was just the same as ever, the first thing that I saw was a taximeter running into a hansom cab. And I took off my hat and cheered. And I went to the Embankment and there was my boat, and the stately river full of dirty, accustomed things. And I rowed back and bought a penny paper, (I had been away it seemed for one day) and I read it from cover to cover—patent remedies for incurable illnesses and all—and I determined to walk, as soon as I was rested, in all the streets that I knew and to call on all the people that I had ever met, and to be content for long with the fields we know.

www.ingramcontent.com/pod-product-compliance
Lightning Source LLC
Chambersburg PA
CBHW050922120626
46552CB00004B/1706

9 781604 507003